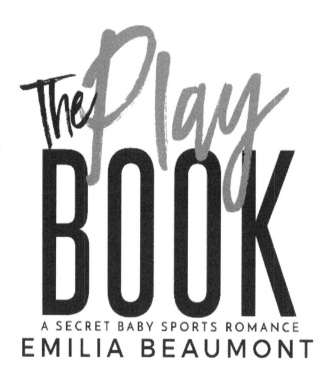

The Play BOOK

A SECRET BABY SPORTS ROMANCE

EMILIA BEAUMONT

* * *

Warning: This novel contains adult situations which may be objectionable to some readers. Not recommended for anyone under the age of 18.

* * *

Want to keep up to date with Emilia's new releases?

Sign up for her newsletter to be the first to know about her new books, promotions and the chance to join her exclusive ebook ARC team!

Newsletter: smarturl.it/BeaumontNewsletter

Website: www.emiliabeaumont.com

Table of Contents

Chapter One
JACOB

She shook her pompoms right in my face and giggled. I was loving every minute of it, catching her nipples and sucking them into my mouth with a greedy slurp at every swinging opportunity. Lovely. Dark and ripe, with a nub that was just begging to be nibbled on.

This was how stars were meant to be treated. And too right, I was a fucking star. Bring on the women, the sex, the alcohol when the coach wasn't looking, not to mention the adoring fans who would be waiting for my arrival. But I wouldn't make the same mistake I made the last time— this time I'd do it right. I'd concentrate on my game… the rest? They would be my side courses; tasters that I would indulge in occasionally.

But who could say no to a little indulgence right now? Especially when the cheerleader was just begging me to devour her right there in the limo.

The tiny uniform top had been stretched to the max up and over her cleavage, revealing the glorious view that swung before me. Her tits wildly batted my stubble-flecked cheeks as I buried my face between them.

This was heaven.

It didn't top scoring a winning touchdown, but it came awfully close.

I couldn't tell you her name—or the other one's, for that matter. The second cheerleader had stripped herself bare as soon as I'd climbed into the limo and was lying upon the long leather seat directly opposite. Without taking her eyes off me she strummed a finger over her glistening clit as she watched her playmate dry-hump me. If I was being truthful, I didn't really care about finding out their names, and I doubted either of them gave a fuck. Especially considering the way Juggs here ground her pussy against me. She was fucking ready for it. Eager and very willing. Who could blame her? I was Jacob Maddox. I was hot fucking stuff.

Straddled across my lap, Juggs pressed her knees into the soft leather of the limo's back seats, and I cupped her ass to bring her closer. Her tight—and no doubt already drenched—gym shorts rubbed hard against my straining cock.

"We're getting close I think. We might have to be quick," I moaned as her pussy took another torturous pass over the bulge in my pants.

"But I don't want it to be quick, Jakey," she said with a cherry-lipped pout. The nickname she assigned me grated on my nerves, but I pushed it away and concentrated on her more appealing qualities instead.

The plan to arrive in a limo with cheerleaders on my arms was a pure media stunt put on by the team's PR department. I think they did it with every player, married or not. Why they thought it was a good idea, I didn't know... but I wasn't thinking straight at that stage anyway. All I had on my mind was sinking myself deep into not one but both of these gifts they'd so generously given me.

The driver had picked me up at the team's temporary housing for incoming players, with the cheerleaders already *in situ* on the back seat. They were gagging for it. They pulled me in and got right to work, unbuckling my belt before I had time to register what was going on. The limo was to drive into the stadium for the press conference and to greet the awaiting fans; it had all been set up for my arrival. It was pure bullshit and I hated the press, but I couldn't complain about the little bonuses.

"Too bad, beggars can't be choosers," I replied and pulled her gym shorts to the side.

She frowned at the word. "I ain't a beggar!"

"Really?" My mouth twisted into a sly grin as I pressed the tip of my finger against her wet seam. She was delightfully smooth, and I couldn't wait to get a taste. My finger slipped between her lips, and she let out an impatient moan. I lifted my hips a fraction, letting her feel what could be inside her if only she'd say the magic words. Juggs tried to sink down upon my pressing finger while her hands did their best to seek out my zipper, but by keeping one hand on her side I rendered her immobile.

Juggs let out another moan and worried her lip. She was in exquisite torture, needing me, wanting me. And yet I had all the power in my hands. Moving my finger a fraction, stroking her, she tilted her head back and cried out again.

"Oh, God. Please, Jakey. Yes, fuck me."

"Do it," the spread-eagled girl across from me said, her tongue darting out to take a swipe at her lips. "Stick it in her. Let me see you fuck her pussy."

Not wanting to disappoint either of them, my fingers quickly sought her out again, spread her wide and thrust into her from behind. I watched Juggs' face—she delighted in being filled, but at the same time her forehead creased with slight disappointed when she realized the two fingers that moved inside her were not the cock she craved.

Spread-eagle squealed as she witnessed her friend getting finger-fucked, her own finger plunging deeper into her sweet cunt. She tugged upon her breast and clamped her nipple between her thumb and forefinger. She gasped, which only encouraged my fingers to piston in and out of her friend's tight hole even harder. The rise in my pants stiffened even more, becoming unbearable. I needed to let the big guy loose.

Visions of what was to come crossed my mind. I would have them both eventually, of course, but first I'd get Juggs on the floor, tits up. She'd lean her head against the bottom cushion of the seat where her friend was stationed, and with me on top she would enjoy my cock. I'd pull Spread-eagle wider and get as close as I could, her legs on either side of her friend, and she would have my tongue to contend with. I couldn't wait and sought my zipper…

Two taps on the passenger window cut through

the escalating moans from both cheerleaders, but it didn't stop Juggs from writhing up and down upon my digits. "No," she whispered, as we both realized the limo had come to a stop. A glance out the tinted window told me we were no longer alone. A small crowd was gathered around the entrance of the stadium… waiting for yours truly.

"Fuck." This couldn't be happening.

I scowled in the direction of the front of the car; the privacy window was still up. But what was the driver thinking? Had he taken the express route to the stadium? He could've at least done me a solid and driven around a few more laps.

"Fuck! Fuck!" I repeated and willed my pulsing erection away, but that was easier said than done when there were two beautiful women waiting to be reamed. Shit, I was about to give myself a severe case of blue-balls, but this was supposedly the time to turn over a new leaf, I reminded myself; duty called.

Knowing she was about to be let down, Juggs tried to clench her legs together to keep my fingers inside. "But I'm so close," she whined as I pulled my hand free and slapped her rump.

"Sorry, Juggs. You two will have to finish yourselves off. I've gotta go to work."

I eased her off my lap, and she landed on the

leather seat with a soft whomp. "It's Izzy!" she cried at me as I hurried to tidy myself up, fastening my belt and straightening my tie.

"Rain check?" I said with a wink, and she just huffed at me and looked away. In their state of undress they wouldn't be making the walk with me, and I turned to the door. "You," I said to Spread-eagle, "I hope I get the chance to play with you properly." She bit her lip and nodded, her fingers never leaving her pussy. "Anytime, honey. Come here, Izzy, let me kiss it better."

Torture.

Pure torture it was, leaving those two, I thought, as I watched Izzy move over to her friend, their hands now wandering over each other's bodies. I swallowed the huge lump in my throat and was about to shout at the chauffeur to drive the fuck away, but a second impatient and louder knock came at the window, and I pushed the impulse aside.

The sound of actual pompoms being shaken, thousands of vinyl strands creating a rustling din, brought a coy smile to my face as I opened the car door to reveal more bouncy-smiley cheerleaders. Each was as lovely as the next, lining the walk from the car to the stadium. God I loved my job, I thought, as I took in all the wondrous flavors of women I knew I would get to sample soon.

Like all the different varieties of ice cream in the world, I was determined to lick each one.

Reporters were also gathered to the side but farther back, their microphones ready to get a word from the newest quarterback to join the Jupiter Suns. I thought I had struck gold when I'd been traded to a Florida team of all things, sun and bikini babes immediately coming to mind. It almost helped overcome the fact that I was a fucking second string quarterback. That was only going to be temporary, though. I was going to outshine the current quarterback and get back a starting position, no matter what... Piece of cake.

Pasting on my killer smile, I stepped out of the car and straightened my suit jacket, coughed and quickly adjusted myself down below, hoping that my hard-on wouldn't be all that noticeable in the commotion. But who was I kidding? It would take a huge moon to eclipse this almighty erection. A couple of the cheerleaders who were close to me in the line smiled a little wider, their eyes dipping to my crotch and then flashing with excitement. One by one, as I advanced through them, like falling dominos at my feet, their cheeks turned a pleasant dusky rose, betraying each and every one of their horny desires for me. I had to admit it—I was pleased I still had what it took to make those panties wet.

Blondes, brunettes, and redheads with eager smiles and bad-ass bodies pressed up against me, and I couldn't resist putting my arms around two of them, as was originally intended, and beamed for the flashing cameras.

"This is the kind of welcome any player would love," I joked with the crowd, earning a few jealous chuckles from the male reporters. I was the new guy in town, but I wasn't immune to the fact that I was needed here. I was going to show everyone that I could play and do it well. And by the end of the season, my performance in Minnesota would be a distant memory. Everyone would've forgotten about the little blip on my score sheet.

"Jacob! How does it feel to be a backup?"

I fought the urge to frown as the camera was shoved in my face, keeping my smile pinned on like a struggling butterfly on a mounting board. "Well," I started, my arms still around two beauties, "I plan to show you all what I can do for the team, and maybe I won't be a backup for long."

Hidden from view, long fingers tipped with acrylic nails grazed over my ass and gave it a slight squeeze, reinvigorating my erection. The cheerleader on my right arm leaned in closer than I thought was possible and whispered into my ear, "You can be my number one any day."

"Have you improved your throwing arm in the off season?" another reporter asked, further stirring the pot. I coughed and tried to control myself, in more ways than one, but was glad for the distraction. It probably wouldn't do me any good to fucking cum right there in my pants. And normally I would have gone off on the reporter, but this was a new team, a new chance, and I needed to make a good impression, even though the women and reporters were both making it hard for me to stick to this new and improved Jacob Maddox. Not to mention, my bank balance couldn't afford another setback.

"It's better than ever," I responded, turning away from the cameras, hoping to be done with them for now.

Up ahead the operations manager waited and nodded the ok to leave the reporters behind. He gave me a serious smile as I approached him. "Jacob, it's good to have you here," he said, outstretching his hand toward me. "Let's get you all settled in, shall we?"

I looked at the women on either side of me, giving them another grin. "Sorry, ladies, but don't go too far, you hear?"

They both giggled in response, and I reluctantly

released them, turning back toward the manager. A tall woman—the shape of an hourglass that even Jessica Rabbit would envy—appeared next to him, her hands crossed over her large chest as she gave me a disapproving look. She took the time to look me up and down, scrutinizing every inch of me, and stopped momentarily as she slowed over my crotch. The outline of yours truly was still very present and noticeable. *Eyes up here, lady.* She let out a tiny gasp but quickly caught herself, her eyes darting away in apparent embarrassment. I chuckled. The corners of my lips naturally turned upwards, and though I had no idea who she was, I gave her a cheeky wink. Ladies loved it when I did that. But this one— fuck, it had no good effect on her. Her scowl deepened, her earlier embarrassment doubled, and a storm brewed in those wild eyes. That was all I needed to see to know she would be a fucking hellcat in bed.

She fidgeted, no longer looking at me… looking everywhere but me if I were being honest. Fuck, I loved it when they got flustered around me.

"John, don't forget to bring him by my office. We have a standing appointment."

"Of course, after we get him all settled in, you know," the manager replied, giving her a harsh stare, then rolling his eyes as he turned back to me. She sniffed. I watched as she debated about saying more, but then she nodded. Whether it was to herself of the manager, I wasn't sure; either way she'd decided not to press the issue. She turned away as John clapped me on the shoulder, pushing me forward through the gate. "Come on, Jacob, let's get you in familiar territory."

* * *

Together we walked through the gate—security shutting it with a clank not long after we were through—and down a newly-laid brick path that ran alongside the stadium's outer walls. As we passed by the public entrances, huge arches that would inevitably lead to the thousands upon thousands of seats within, I was able to catch a sliver of a glimpse of the field.

"Wanna take a look?" John asked, and I nodded eagerly.

Under the Florida sun the field glistened, the grass was pristine, the lines were startling white and crisp. Leaning against a cold rail, I breathed it all in. The place was empty, but there was something akin to a soul lingering in the stadium, like it almost breathed with me. I loved the potential of a new field, especially the first game of the season, the way my cleats sank into the turf as I set my stance to make a big play. There was no other feeling like it, the scoreboard set at zero with everything to play for. But now I was going to be fighting to even get onto the field this season.

I hated the uncertainty—the damage it had done to my pride. The serenity that I'd felt earlier in my career was stripped away. But it left me even more determined not to fuck up or to let others fuck it up for me again.

I was not washed up. I was not done with this sport, no matter what they said on the TV and radio. I was going to show them exactly what I was made of, and by the end of the fucking season, so help me God, the whole world would know my name.

"C'mon, we better get going. The team is here today out on the practice fields," John was saying. "I would like for you to meet them and then get you started if you're up for sweating a little bit on your first day. We can get some reps in, get a true feel for your style, and let you meet Danny."

"Sure," I replied confidently, "no time like the present." Danny Miller was my competition, the starting quarterback, and I wanted to know everything about him—his weaknesses, his strengths, anything that could potentially give me a leg up and help me make my dreams come true. It was ruthless to think that way about a teammate, but he was getting on; it was time he let a new guy take over.

We found our way back outside, and John commandeered a cart that would take us around the back of the main stadium. He drove us into a second gated area, practice fields on either side. There was a stout-looking three-story building up ahead, plain, but in the same style as its bigger brother that we'd just come from. Glass and concrete were married together in perfect harmony, with familiar archways that lined the facade. John eased the cart up in front, and we hopped off.

He first escorted me through the building's office-like interior—practical but with modern flourishes here and there—and then as he led me down what I presumed to be the main tunnel, which would eventually lead back out to the practice fields, I started to get chills. Anticipation, nerves, and everything in between were building up like a coiled spring within me. And of course it hadn't helped that I was ready to bust a nut, too. But this was it, this was to be my home for the foreseeable future, and a familiar sense of pressure weighed down upon me.

We took a turn off the tunnel and into a room that blasted out air conditioning, the sudden drop in temperature causing the chills to turn to shivers. We walked through a final set of glass doors and into a large locker room, the carpet plush under my feet. Rows of large, open lockers completed a semi-circle, each of them painted in the team's colors and labeled with a name. Glancing at each one of them, I immediately started to look for my own name but found it nowhere.

"Your locker is this way," John said, sensing my question. I cleared my throat and walked past the first row of lockers to the second row, clearly separated from the starters. Hell, I was second even in the locker room! It was to be expected, of course, I just didn't realize how much of a gut-punch it would actually be.

A few of the guys noticed us, pausing in their preparation for practice as I passed by. I kept my smile, clenching my jaw tight, nodding to a few of them as John led me to my locker. *On the second fucking row.* I didn't belong there, but I didn't plan on being there for long.

"I'll let you get settled in; the boys will soon introduce themselves," he was saying, giving me a nervous smile. "If you need anything, just holler, Jacob. We are glad you're here."

"I'm glad to be here, too," I forced out. He nodded, and I turned to the locker, removed my jacket, and hung it up.

Sitting at the bottom of the locker, all ready for me, was a set of all new practice gear, emblazoned with the team's logo. No longer was I wearing the gold and green that I had worn in my first year. Now my colors were blue and yellow, a dazzling sun with sharp rays as my logo. It was going to take some getting used to. When I had signed my first NFL contract, I'd expected to be with the team for the entire five years... longer if possible. I'd imagined a long and loyal career. Instead, I'd carried the program to a two-and-fourteen loss, throwing more interceptions than anyone else in the entire league. Though every player had the fear of a trade in the back of his mind, I had no idea that it was going to come as quickly as it had.

"Hey, you're Jacob Maddox."

I turned to see a young guy next to me, an eager smile on his face. "Dude, I heard you were coming, but I didn't believe them. Terrence, Terrence Gold. I'll be your wide receiver."

"Terrence, nice to meet ya," I said, sticking out my hand. "Second string?"

"You know it," he laughed, shaking my hand. "At least it's not third. Hell, I'm just glad to be on the team, you know?"

"Yeah, well, second isn't good enough for me," I grumbled, releasing his tight grip. "I'll be a starter before the end of this season, you watch."

"Good luck with that. Danny's on fire. In the zone," Terrence answered absently as he reached into his locker. I watched as he tidied away a shirt and inadvertently pushed forward a small black object against the side. The thing fell down with a flutter onto the floor. "Shit," he said, looking down. "Dude, can you grab that for me?"

Not wanting to make an enemy right off the bat, I reached down and picked up the object for him like he asked, and I realized it was a little book, almost Bible-like. Small and thick. But this one didn't have the delicate flimsy pages of a Bible; it was, on second glance, just a normal, everyday ledger. Come to think of it, it looked lot like a little black book. Terrence was still busy, and I chanced a peek. Opening it up, I thumbed through the pages. There was writing on practically every page, but there was an undecipherable code alongside it. "What's this? What does this number mean?"

"Aw man it's… shit, just give it back." He was trying to a hide a smile but wasn't doing a good job at it.

"What is it? Let me in on the secret," I said and took a step out of his reach as he tried to snatch it from me. It was a feeble attempt, and I easily dodged him.

"Fine. It's, you know, one of those books," he

replied, giving me a light punch on the shoulder. "Every woman that has ever been with one of the players is tagged in there."

"Tagged?" I frowned trying to get his meaning and stopped to read one of the entries.

Number twelve, banging body. Ginger likes it rough. Pull her hair during doggie style and she will do the big o. It was signed with a number—twenty-four, a jersey number?—and what looked to be a date from last year beside it. Looking up at Terrence, I pointed at the entry.

"You can't be serious!" It was something that teenagers did in high school, not grown men worth millions of dollars, but I had to admit, it did have an element of fun to it.

"Don't give me that look. I know you're a total player if last year's gossip rags are anything to go by. But seriously, dude, it's the best thing ever," Terrence said, almost bouncing on his heels. "You can find any girl you want in there; those that like it rough or easy, exhibitionists, ones that are like the girl next door, or even a dom if you're into that kinky shit. I tell you that playbook has made many men extremely happy."

"Playbook?" I said with an amused shake of my head. It was a good name—immature, but genius at the same time, especially considering the men using it. Even I had to see the brilliance in that.

I flipped through the remaining pages, a big red X catching my eye. "What's up with this one? There's no jersey number," I asked, pointing to the entry.

Lucia the Untouchable. Wants a ring on that finger before she will pay out. Hates everyone, especially players. Doesn't like to be touched. Won't flirt... Don't even fucking try.

The entry continued in different handwriting beneath the first.

More like the Unfuckable! The Ice Queen reigns supreme!

"Oh, man, that's Lucia," Terrence replied, swallowing hard as he looked at the entry. "Like it says on the score sheet, she's not worth your time or any other man's, for that matter. Strictly off limits."

"What's wrong with her?" I asked, my curiosity piqued as I continued to look at the long list of things that Lucia didn't like. Not one entry was positive.

"Nothing's wrong with her physically... Bangin' body, if I'm to be honest, slammin' curves in all the right places," Terrence said with a sigh, pulling the book out of my hands. "She's just one of those all-business types, you know? Won't go near jocks. Trust me, there's no point even trying.

She's a lost cause. If you're interested, better to go for a guaranteed lay. Less hassle." Terrence threw the book back into the locker and grabbed his cleats. "Come on, get changed. I'll show you the practice field."

With a lingering look at the small black playbook, I started to get undressed. No one had resisted my charms before, and I doubted this Lucia would be any different. Don't even try? We'll see about that.

Chapter Two
LUCIA

My heels sank into the deep carpet as I walked down the hall, my mind always going back to why anyone would put carpeting where sweaty men will drip on it. *Eugh,* it was disgusting—they really needed to get it replaced. This type of carpet belonged in a nice house, not a football training building. Most of the men had already made it out to the practice field, but as I rounded the corner, I saw two guys huddled together near the therapy room, heads together, reminding me of schoolgirls talking about their crushes.

"Dude, he totally bought it. We are going to have some fun with this one."

The other chuckled and shook his head, his

tight braids sliding back and forth on his practice jersey. "I can't believe that. Are you sure it's going to go down tonight?"

I frowned, wondering what they could be talking about. Pranks were a common theme in the locker room, the guys enjoying a chance to blow off some steam from the stress of performing. I had seen numerous ones over the years, even been the butt of some harmless ones last year. But none ever got out of control or harmed anyone. Putting my best strict teacher face on, one that I had perfected to keep unruly clients in check, I put my hands on my hips and cleared my throat. "Guys, I hope you aren't planning to do something you are going to regret?"

At the sound of my voice, they turned quickly, both of them looking guilty as hell that they were caught slacking off. Like two little boys who'd been caught stealing cookies, they bolted upright with hands behind their backs, a small flash of black disappearing as they did so. They certainly were not acting like twenty-something year-old men who made millions of dollars a year. "Ms. Cortes, we weren't doing nothing."

"Sure," I said, holding their stares. "Who's the unlucky soul this time? You better not be hazing another cheerleader again, or I will have your balls, gentlemen."

One of them looked away, guilt written all over his face. The other, Terrence—a running back if I remembered correctly—cleared his throat and gave me a smile, one that normally would melt the panties off a girl. Not me; I was too used to it. I'd been around guys like this all my life. I knew every cocky smile, every twinkling wink and every muscle-bulging move they used to sway women to their side.

"We were just talking. You know, guy talk."

I smiled knowingly, crossing my arms over my chest. "Is that right? Well if you like to talk so much, Terrence, you could have made your last appointment with me."

The other guy snickered, and Terrence averted his gaze, his winning smile fading. I'd inadvertently embarrassed him.

"Lucia! What the hell are you doing?"

I turned around to find the head coach, Greg Hanshield, staring me down, his hands on his hips. Greg was in his fifteenth year as coach of the Jupiter Suns, his record better than most.

"How can I help you, Greg?"

He walked toward me, his pot belly leading the way, looking over my shoulder at the two players still standing there.

"Are you harassing my players? It's the damn start of the season, Lucia. They don't have time for your mumbo jumbo!"

Mumbo jumbo? He had a nerve! I hated that he thought I was some kind of sideshow attraction. Why couldn't he understand that I was a professional, just like him, here to make a difference?

"Excuse me? I wasn't harassing them."

"Sure sounded like it to me," Greg grumbled, the stink of his body odor becoming increasingly suffocating. "Your daddy would hate to hear that you were keeping his players from doing their jobs."

I swallowed a retort that was on the tip of my tongue. He knew bringing up my father would stop me in my tracks, and I hated that it had that effect on me. I started to count to ten, trying to let the anger dissipate. Why I ever thought taking a job here would be a good idea, I didn't know.

Greg, picking up on my rising anger, sneered at me, knowing he'd won this round. "Why don't you run along and go play therapist like your daddy expects you to, Lucia. Leave the real work to the professionals."

The two players snickered, and Greg turned on

them, his grin evaporating. "Get the hell out of here before I make you both run until you pass out!" The two players turned and hightailed it out of the hall, leaving just Greg and me there. He turned back to me, his smirk not at all friendly. "Now Lucia, I know you think you rule the roost around here, but one word from me to your daddy, and he will pull you out faster than I can snap my fingers." Taking a step forward, he leaned in so that I could be the only one to hear his words, even though we were alone. "Do not fucking harass my players, or else."

My fists felt like they wanted to fly; I wanted to hit him so bad I could taste it. But if I did, it wouldn't solve anything—Greg would get what he'd wanted since last year: me out on my ear and his precious players left with a myriad of mental health issues. Not that he wanted that last part of course, he was just oblivious to their psychological needs.

Drumming up as much willpower as I could, I spun on my heel and started to walk away, but upon hearing his laughter, I called back, "Oh, by the way, Greg? You stink."

Enjoying the tiny victory, I stayed only long enough to see the smirk slip off his face as his nose instinctively dipped downwards towards his sweat-laden armpit.

My office was situated at the end of the long hall, with close access to the locker room so the players could visit me at any time should they need to. Not that they did. With assholes like Greg Hanshield on the coaching staff, they tended to shy away from me except for their mandatory therapy sessions that I'd pushed for with my father.

Slamming the door, I crossed over to my desk and fell into the chair, rage bubbling at the surface. The way I had just been treated made me want to scream. I'd been the Jupiter Suns' performance therapist for a little over a year. My master's degree in psychology hung proudly on the wall in front of me, but you'd think it was a blank piece of paper if you went by the staff's reactions to my presence.

When I finished school, I'd expected to be bombarded with offers, but of course times were tight and there wasn't much call for my specialization. Waiting on pins and needles, I'd applied for every job I thought I could do, but when nothing was forthcoming, my father stepped in. He offered to make me part of the franchise, a therapist to help the guys with any mental struggles they had and to just give them someone to talk to. And with all the pressure they experienced, I jumped at the chance, thrilled to finally apply what I had learned. I thought I'd be turning players away, but no such luck. Even so, I had to admit my position, effectively working for my dad, was incredibly fortuitous. Yet now, after what seemed like years of hazing, I was tempted to throw in the towel.

I looked down at my carefully constructed—but mostly empty—day-planner on my desk, seeing that I had the newest member of the team, Jacob Maddox, scheduled within the hour. Regardless of my thoughts of quitting, I knew I couldn't bail—today was not that day. I tapped my pen against the desk, thinking how I could make our first session a success. Perhaps a change in my method was needed.

He was a second string quarterback that my father picked up to help offload some of the stress on his star quarterback, Danny Miller. It should have been a good choice, but from my own research into his background (it would be a cold day in hell before the coaches shared their notes on their players with me), I knew that Jacob had struggled last season, his team ending up at the bottom of the entire league. *That, quite possibly, could be something Jacob needs to deal with*, I mused. In fact, I remembered that my father had been the butt of many jokes for signing him. And more than once I'd heard him cussing out his operations manager for putting him in such a situation. The Jupiter Suns had a chance at a good season this year, and someone coming in with a great deal of baggage tied to his name was going to be a burden they really didn't need.

Leaning back in my chair, I thought about Jacob Maddox' arrival earlier, the way he had allowed the cheerleaders to drape all over him like he was a celebrity. I had to admit, he was insanely cute up close, his thick brown hair barely brushing the collar of his suit jacket, and his dazzling blue eyes reminding me of a clear summer's day. There was a mischievousness to them, like he knew exactly what you were thinking, and he was going to tell the whole world.

His smile, well, it was the kind that would make a woman involuntarily moan out loud, and I could tell he knew how to use it to his advantage. Another flash of that winning smile, and I knew my heart would race uncontrollably again—just like it had done earlier. I thought I was going to faint when he noticed me looking at his bulging crotch. The result of having all those women wrapped around him no doubt, I thought spitefully, wishing that I could have that effect on someone. I never thought I'd be jealous of how close they were to him, but cheerleaders had all the fun.

"Quit it, Lucia," I scolded myself, shaking my head clear of any other musings about the new, hot, and very lickable player. What was wrong with me? I had lost all of my good common sense. He was going to be my patient. I was a professional, and professionals did not fantasize about good-looking football players.

What on earth was I thinking? He was a player—off limits—and long ago, I had decided that I wanted nothing to do with jocks of any kind. They never took anything seriously. And even though some of them were down-to-earth, married with cute kids, it had never even crossed my mind to become a player's wife, let alone girlfriend, most of whom were forced to be alone or single parents during the football season. I knew for a fact that most of these guys saw their families or significant others only once or twice during the week when they were training, less during the season itself. Nowadays, their off season was so short, too, since they made appearances for charity and such as representatives of the team.

I couldn't do that. I wouldn't do that. I was on the verge of making my own career take off and to have it occupied by another person was not going to happen… I didn't slave through six years of college just to have someone overshadow what I wanted to accomplish. And yet, there was still that little voice in my head that said it might be nice to share those things with someone else.

No. I was fine. My way—keeping my head down, absorbed in my work—hadn't failed me thus far, so why even try something new?

Bracing my hands on the desk, I grabbed a stack of files that needed to be dictated into my extensive records. I had to keep my head in the game, no pun intended. I was here for a reason, and it wasn't to ogle over the new players, even if the upcoming meeting with a certain quarterback was making my stomach flutter with a thousand anxious butterflies.

Chapter Three
JACOB

I climbed out of the SUV and put on a smile. My body ached in a good way from the brutal practice session. Being used to the first string, I'd been abruptly introduced to the second string practice, meaning that I was actually on the field, throwing the ball as the first string defense practiced. My ribs still hurt from where I'd been drilled into the turf by a quick-footed defensive back. Trey had stood over me with a pleased grin and welcomed me officially to the team. Not even a dip in the ice tub had taken away the sting, and I was sure I would have some bruises blooming in the morning. The experience certainly wasn't what I was used to, but I didn't plan on it staying that way for long. Somehow, some way, I was going to get to first string.

Still, my first day had gone pretty well overall. A handful of my new team members, Terrence included, invited me out with them for some much needed downtime. He had been the one to pick me up from the team's temporary housing, where I was currently based until I could find a more permanent place to live, then bringing me to a local—bordering on fancy—restaurant where the team enjoyed having dinner. They even had a reserved room in the back with a complete buffet and full bar waiting for us on our arrival. That wasn't the only thing waiting.

"Dude, see? I bet you didn't have anything like this in Minnesota," Terrence was saying as we entered the room. Women were everywhere, outnumbering the men two to one. Some had sparkling diamonds on their fingers, and I knew they were off limits, the wives of some of the players who hadn't fallen victim to the whole family thing yet. But there were plenty of spare women whose ring fingers were unoccupied. I put on my dazzling smile, perfect for the occasion, one that the ladies couldn't resist. I wouldn't be going home alone tonight.

Walking over to the bar, I ordered a beer and enjoyed the view, catching the eye of a blonde in the corner who was pretending not to pay attention to me. She was gorgeous, a slight smile playing on her luscious red lips. Every man's instant hard-on, but for me, well, I really didn't have a type. I liked them all, regardless of hair or skin color. While I preferred a woman who was shorter than me, my last real girlfriend—a runway model—was a few inches taller, especially when she wore a set of killer heels. Just thinking about those heels being worn to bed and the blonde giving me the fuck-me eyes made the bulge in my pants increasingly hard.

When I thought about it, it had been way too long since I'd had a woman in my actual bed (occasional backseat blow-jobs and quickies didn't really count). I'd been too consumed with the mess of my professional career that had led me to this place. My ex had split as soon as the waters of my life got rough—another woman looking only for the glitz and glamour of dating a professional athlete. I couldn't blame her, though. I wasn't the type to stick around when the going got tough in a relationship, either. I liked the good and fun times but not the emotional side that sucked people into thinking that love was forever and all that shit.

"See? Don't we get treated good here?"

I looked up to find Terrence next to me, grinning from ear to ear, his eyes on the bevy of ladies that were milling around the room.

"Yeah," I responded, taking a long draw off my beer. "This is good, man." It was exactly what I needed after this morning's false start.

Trey joined us, swaying as he walked up to the bar. His eyes were already starting to glaze over. He threw his massive arm around my shoulders, giving me a friendly squeeze. "Dude, I can't believe I tackled you so hard today. I guess I was pumped. I'm just fucking ready to get this season started."

I felt the pull of my ribs and smiled uncomfortably, knowing I would remember him for days to come. "Hey, no problem, Trey. It's a brutal sport." I doubted the big guy would be apologizing to me if he weren't already three sheets to the wind, the smell of whiskey strong on his breath.

"I feel so bad, man," the big guy continued, "Lemme buy you a drink."

"Better yet, Trey," Terrence interrupted with a grin, "why don't you tell Jacob here your favorite number in the playbook. We need to get the new guy laid."

"The book," Trey repeated, a similar grin coming over his face as he released me. "Hell yeah, that's what I can do for you. I can get you someone gooood. That will make up for my hit, though it was a damn fine hit."

"I… no thanks," I replied, my thoughts drifting back to earlier in the day. There was only one name that had stuck out to me in that book, the one with the fat red X. *A real challenge.* I didn't know why, but I was highly intrigued. She seemed like a woman who was looking to be conquered, and I could be… no, I *was* that man. Besides, I was perfectly capable of pulling chicks on my own.

"Come on, Jacob," Terrence said, slapping me on the back with a friendly laugh. "Which one do you want? Red-head? Blonde? There are some real gems in that book, some that will knock your socks off." He then grinned—toothy and wide—and gave Trey a wink. "Get it? Knock your socks off?" Trey laughed, though I doubted he had gotten the joke; his face was looking pale now. How much alcohol could that man hold, anyway? Eager not to get puked on, I stepped casually to the side… just in case.

"Think of it as our welcome present to you," Terrence finished, a smile in his voice. "A proper welcome to the team type of thang."

I rubbed the back of my neck, wishing that I could just get drunk and pound away at one of these women at the end of the night, but my thoughts kept straying back to Madam X, Lucia. Now if she was really an untouchable woman, I wanted to be the one to touch her.

These guys would go fucking crazy if I could and I would have no problem gaining their respect. Hell, it might even get me to that starting position in the long run. A man who had the team behind him was a powerful one; a leader they would follow. "I want Lucia then."

Trey took one look at Terrence and they both burst into laughter. "You want the unfuckable? Terrence, didn't you tell him about her? Hell naw, man, you don't want her. Are you crazy? Don't stick your dick in crazy, man."

"I did tell him," Terrence said defensively, giving me an odd look like he couldn't believe what I was saying. "She's… not for you. There's no way you will get within ten feet of her, anyway. She'll walk all over you in a minute, dude."

"You wanna bet?" I asked, raising a brow. Hell, there weren't many women that could turn me down. There had been only one if I was remembering correctly: Sarah from eighth grade, but that was only because she was moving away. I still got a peck on the cheek, though, as my goodbye present. Turning on the Jacob Maddox charm was second nature to me, and now, with a whole new population to tackle, I wanted to start with the hardest one. I wanted a challenge, just like on the field where I performed to my highest caliber. This would get me started off on the right foot here in this town.

"I bet I can get in her bed before the season is over. She will be panting after me like a dog with a bone."

Trey leaned in close, his eyes looking into mine. "Hey, Terrence, I think I hit him too hard today. You think he's got a concussion?"

"He's gonna have one if he goes after her," Terrence answered. "Face it, Jacob, you will lose the bet before it ever really begins with that one. No one gets anywhere with Lucia except in trouble. She's a tough broad."

"A grand says otherwise," I replied confidently, draining the rest of my beer. "To both of you if I lose. Come on, take a chance. If I fall on my face, you will be a grand richer, both of you."

"Aw, hell, he's breaking out the big guns," Terrence laughed, eyeing me. "Okay fine, I'm in. Daddy needs a new pair of shoes."

"Me too," Trey said, banging on the bar with his burly hands. "Hey, let's get a round of shots here! We got some toasting to do!"

I shook my head and looked at my newfound friends. They really had no idea how good I was at winning over women… I had just won over both of them, and the night wasn't even done yet.

"I tell you what," Terrence said, throwing an arm over my shoulders after we downed a round of shots. "You should get started tonight. She works late hours at the facility."

"She works at the stadium? For the team?" I asked, surprised. Was it really going to be that easy? I thought I was going to have to figure out who she was exactly, but a job at the stadium? Hell, that solved all my problems. She would be in close proximity to yours truly, making it even harder to resist me.

"Yeah, didn't I mention that? She practically lives there," Trey said, handing me another shot of tequila. "Maybe if you're man enough, you could win the bet tonight."

I thought about it for a moment, a wary grin spreading over my face. He was a little too eager, so it was probably too good to be true. But I wasn't about to back down now. I wanted her. And the idea of knocking it out of the park tonight would truly put me in good stead with them.

She would never know what hit her, and by the time she did, I would be buried so deep that she wouldn't want me to get out.

"All right," I said, raising my glass. "Some Dutch courage and I'll go get her." This was going to be the easiest bet I'd ever won.

Chapter Four
LUCIA

I stepped off the elliptical, wiping my face with the towel. I enjoyed this time of the evening, when the stadium, training grounds, and offices were quiet and no one else was around. It was therapeutic, a time when I could go over my day and prepare for the next. And while the job didn't need me to stay so late—especially with my sad lack of patients—I still preferred to stick around till after everyone else went home.

The empty gym was certainly a bonus. I could train without feeling embarrassed, huffing and puffing. But it had done wonders for my fitness levels, though I was never going to be a bean pole; my curves were here to stay. Besides going home to my parents' guest house and heating up a single microwave dinner never had me rushing for the door. My life consisted of two states: home and work, no real play to speak of. Well, I relaxed with a book occasionally. That was enough excitement for me, or at least that's what I told myself.

Yes, it sounded horribly pathetic but college work had taken up much of my life for the last six years. My best friend lived halfway across the country, and I didn't have any really close friends in Florida. When I had first moved back home, I had dated a time or two, but the guys, once they found out who my father was, seemed to only want to get close to me to get close to him, and I just didn't have the time to put up with that. I really didn't want to. I was too old to want nothing more than the mindless world of dating and sex with random partners. My last real boyfriend had tried to talk me out of pursuing my master's degree, a mistake he had lived to regret. Looking back, I think he was intimidated that I was so professionally driven, so he tried to fit me into that 'little woman' mold that would make me secondary to him. Needless to say, I wasn't disappointed when he packed his stuff up and left.

Sighing, I pushed open the door to the gym and ran smack into a solid wall that smelled like spicy vanilla musk with a hint of malty beer.

"Hey there, I got you." Two warm hands gripped my bare upper arms and held me steady as my own hands landed against a very muscular chest, covered with a smooth dress shirt that I had to resist running my fingers over. A steady heartbeat pounded beneath my hands.

"I am so sorry," I stammered, my mind racing as I pulled back out of the grip and looked upward, expecting to see the janitor or an equipment manager working late. No such luck.

Who I found was a complete surprise. Jacob Maddox was standing before me, a happy grin on his handsome face that had my heart hammering in my chest. Here I was, in my gym shorts and a sports crop-top, dripping with sweat, and he, well, he looked like he had just come from a GQ photo-shoot.

"W-what are you doing here?"

He leaned against the doorway, blocking my path to freedom, his smile growing as he let his eyes slide up and down my body. My legs weakened and my knees trembled the longer his eyes roamed. Suddenly I wanted to be in a short cocktail dress, my curves strapped in and smoothed down. I wished I could look like a vixen, the type of woman I knew he was used to having on his arm.

"I was looking for someone," he responded, his voice a low baritone.

"Oh?" I asked, crossing my arms over my middle in an effort to hide my near nakedness. Goosebumps started to appear up and down my body and they weren't just the result of evaporating sweat. "Who's that?" Breathing him in, I took a step back. Why did he have to smell so good?

"Lucia," he replied with a lopsided smile that sent my heart into overtime. He was looking for me? But why now?

"You wouldn't happen to know who she is, do you?"

Startled, I realized he had no idea who I actually was. So why was he looking for me? Was he going to apologize for not coming to his appointment today? I had been so mad; the entire conversation I was going to have with him had been planned out in my head, but he'd never given me the chance. And now he had caught me at a very vulnerable moment, and I was in no mood to be seen by the gorgeous football player, without even a lick of any makeup on! Plus, I probably smelled like sweaty gym socks. "W-why are you looking for her?" I asked hesitantly, not wanting to reveal myself... at least not yet.

He looked at me for a moment and I could tell by his unfocused, soft eyes that he had been drinking. Great. Now I had a drunk, mouth-watering football player to deal with.

"Well, I dunno if I need to find her now that I have found you. Where have you been all of my life, gorgeous?"

I wanted to laugh, really. He thought I was gorgeous? Jacob Maddox must be smashed, his vision blurred to the point where he couldn't see the sweaty, red-faced woman in front of him. Yes, that had to be it. Intrigued by what he would want with me, I found myself not wanting to leave just yet. Besides, I doubted he would remember this conversation in the morning. If he did, well, our first encounter as client and therapist was going to be very awkward indeed. "Mr. Maddox, you are drunk."

"Nah, just a little tipsy," he said, pressing his fingers together to the point where they were barely touching.

I pursed my lips, trying to remember the last time I had gotten drunk myself. It had been a long, long time ago—a distant memory. Now I'd graduated to just a glass of wine or bottle of beer on the weekends. I hadn't let myself have that type of fun since my first year of college, and I was no longer that girl anymore.

I was responsible and determined, a professional woman.

"So, are you going to be cheering for me on game days, honey?" He continued edging closer to me. "Though if you do, I won't be able to stay focused, knowing you are on the sidelines."

"Are you always so flirty with the help?" I asked, realizing he thought I was a cheerleader. Yeah, right. I had no rhythm nor inclination to shake my ass, or those daft pompoms. And while I tried to take care of my body, I was too blessed in the chest region to be bouncing around the sidelines in one of those tight tops—I would need at least two sports bras to strap down what my mama gave me!

"Well there's no law that says I can't flirt," he answered, reaching out to brush a stray hair from my face without warning.

The mere contact of his fingers left a trail of heat on my cheek, and I sucked in a breath. I knew I should've stopped him before anything else weird happened and simply walk away. But this was the most exciting thing that had happened to me in quite a while; it wasn't every day that a strong, gorgeous man took the time to flirt with me. Why shouldn't I allow myself this bit of fun? No one else was going to know, and I highly doubted that Mr. Maddox was going to remember it in the morning, either. I just hoped he wasn't driving. "N-no, I guess there isn't," I finally said as he dropped his fingers.

"Well then," he replied, pushing off of the doorframe and getting his balance, his feet seemingly unable to cooperate. "I see that you have already worked up a sweat without me. Now that is not fair at all."

He was getting close, far too close, but like his feet, mine didn't want to move, either.

"People tend to do that in the gym," I laughed, finding this conversation absurd but delightful. When was the last time I had talked to anyone who wasn't required to talk to me by a contract or wasn't related to me?

He chuckled, the sound spreading a glow of warmth down into my lower belly. Idly, I wondered what would it be like to be touched properly by him? Besides, wasn't this all just a fantasy anyway? Was he a slow lover, methodical and sure, or was he a fast lover, who liked to be more of a wham, bam, thank you ma'am kind of guy? But why was I putting all of this thought into a guy I barely knew anyway? Was it because he was drunk and I was, well, lonely?

The thought struck me hard. Oh God, I was lonely. Here I was almost twenty-five without anyone in my life save my career… work that did not keep me warm at night. Now, Jacob Maddox, he could definitely keep a girl scorching hot at night, let alone warm.

"What else do you do to work up a sweat?" he asked softly, his eyes twinkling. I laughed nervously and looked away. I could feel the heat spread across my cheeks betraying how much I was enjoying standing there with him. The ache in my lower region intensified.

Jacob took a step forward and I sucked in another breath, my lungs bursting with anticipation. When his hands grasped me around the waist, his fingers touching my bare skin, I nearly gasped aloud as the heat coursed through my body—it was almost overwhelming; the long forgotten touch of a man and the torturous heat he created. He pushed me up against the wall, the coolness of the concrete bricks cold against my back before his lips descended upon mine. I tasted the sweet beer on his lips then froze for a moment—surely I was dreaming? This couldn't very well be happening to me, right now, with him, here at my place of work?

Was he really kissing me, or was I imagining it all? I wasn't too sure which would be worse. That I would be so desperate to conjure up a panty-melting fantasy, or that I was actually kissing a player.

When his lips roamed lazily over mine, I heard myself sigh, my hands drifting up to his broad shoulders, the muscles honed from his long hours on the field. His tongue delved into my mouth; the sweet fire of his tongue touching mine sent sparks down my spine, curling my toes. *Oh my.* I had to stop this. But did I really want to? This was perhaps the hottest kiss I'd had ever had, everything I thought it could be and more. Who could have thought that it would be this mind-blowing? And what the hell had I been missing out on?

The reality of who I was kissing came rushing back to me, full force, like a slap in the face. Jacob Maddox. I was kissing a football player, the one group of men I had sworn off completely. Not only that, I was kissing one that was due to be a patient—even if it was only an introductory meeting, a patient nonetheless. He was also a man I had no earthly idea about, not really. Sure I knew the tabloid playboy version of Jacob Maddox, but in reality I was kissing an absolute stranger. And yet it was delicious.

Pushing at his shoulders, I broke the kiss, forcing him back so that I could get out from under him. With a hand over my mouth I turned away from him, needing to be far, far away before my body persuaded me to do something crazy.

"Hey, wait!" he called as I hurried to the door, "I don't even know your name."

I burst out into laughter, thinking how absurd that was. He did know my name, but he still didn't know that the girl he was looking for and the girl he had just kissed were one and the same.

I got through the door, hurried down the hall and encased myself in my office with the door shut in the span of a few seconds. Thank God we didn't have our names on plaques by our offices, or he would find "Lucia" in ten seconds flat. My hands were shaking, my knees were knocking together, and my heart was racing. I felt like I'd just run a marathon and was about to collapse on the asphalt at the finish line. But standing with my back against the door, as if I were attempting to barricade and deny my feelings, I realized that wasn't the scary part. The scary part was that I wanted to kiss him again… and again.

The dam was broken. Perhaps even irreparable.

What I had I just done? Why hadn't I left at the first glimpse of the man?

With a heavy sigh and with adrenaline still coursing through my body, skin that Jacob Maddox had touched, I pushed off the door in a great hurry. I threw on a spare sweatshirt I had stashed in a drawer, then grabbed my work bag, searching desperately for my keys. I needed to get out of here before Jacob starting his quest again, looking for the elusive *Lucia*.

Chapter Five
JACOB

My head hurt like it had been through five rounds with Tyson. And the phone call I'd just received was the last thing I needed. How he'd gotten my number—I'd changed it so many times—was beyond me. But as soon as I'd heard his voice I hung up and blocked his further attempts. When was he going to get the message that I didn't want anything to do with him?

I thought it would take him longer to find me. I groaned. I was going to have to get a new cell. Instead of dealing with his crap I wanted nothing more than to lie in my bed and recuperate. Not only from the relentless hangover but also from the encounter with the most intriguing woman while looking for the untouchable and unfindable Lucia from the playbook.

While I didn't remember everything about last night, I did remember enough to make me feel bad for the woman I had nearly accosted. Although I still had a bet to win, the searing kiss from my gym bunny had me wondering if I would run into her today at the stadium. I didn't know her name, but I knew the curves of her body, and I just hoped that she wouldn't go running the other way when we finally did meet without the aid of alcohol. I wanted to apologize for my drunken kiss, with the hope that she would let me take her out on a date so that I could end our night with something more fulfilling.

But first, I had to meet with some fucking performance coach or therapist or some shit like that. Today was not the day to be pouring out my feelings to some shrink who couldn't care two fucks about me or my performance. Her voicemail from yesterday afternoon already told me that she wasn't my biggest fan, considering I had missed the first appointment.

"Mr. Maddox, you are required by the contract you signed with the Jupiter Suns to meet with me, and I expect my clients to show up when I schedule them. I further expect to see you in my office at nine a.m., first thing in the morning. Don't be late, or I will be forced to turn in my blank report, which won't be very good for you."

Her tone belied her frustration, but I couldn't help but notice a sexiness behind it. Images of an authoritative woman in killer heels standing ready to dress me down in the bedroom had my cock standing at attention. *Shit.* Her voice was starting to get me hard, and that didn't bode well for the meeting that morning. I needed to get laid and soon, before I started humping the first thing in sight.

I pulled the car up to the stadium and parked in the players' parking lot, wincing as I opened the door and climbed out into the bright sunshine. That was one thing I was already missing about Minnesota. In a hangover situation, it was nice to have a cloudy, overcast day instead of one that felt like it was driving dazzling spears into my eyes. My sunglasses didn't even block out the rays; they pierced them, making my head throb.

Thankfully it wasn't long before I was walking into the air-conditioned building and down the hall, my thoughts returning to the foolish bet I'd made with the guys. A little bit of alcohol in me and I thought I could do anything—well, I couldn't back down now. I had to find this Lucia character so I could start wooing her and win two grand and my teammates' respect. I had doubts that she was as tough as the book made her out to be. No woman could resist a winning smile and some smooth talking. I just had to find her so she could experience the Maddox charm. She was a challenge I was more than willing to handle.

Looking down at my watch, I realized I was already thirty minutes late for this stupid appointment. Clearly I was not going to be the therapist's favorite player on the team, but nor did I care to be. All I really wanted to do was go back and bury my head in my covers for the rest of the day. Actually I wanted to bury myself into something else, but the gym bunny last night had been my only chance that evening. And after her rejection, instead of going back to the guys as a failure, I had made my way to the player's digs somehow, passing out across the king-sized bed alone.

I found the office number and walked in, stopping in my tracks at the sight before me. The performance sports therapist, or at least I presumed it was her, was standing on a chair, her very shapely ass encased in a tight pencil skirt that was about eye-level across from me. Her legs were long and shapely and her body stretched out as she attempted to hoist some books onto a top shelf behind her desk. I couldn't help but admire the view, taking in her wavy but tight frame as she stretched. God, what a sight. Every part of me, including my cock, was waving a thunderous hello, definitely not expecting the doctor to be such a looker from behind.

Loving the cock-teasing show, I leaned against the doorway, watching as she moved the books around on the shelf, her ass wiggling in the process, before I took in the rest of her small but tidy office. On the opposite wall there were numerous certificates encased in solid wood frames. So the doc was a smart one, go figure. The only certificate I had was my high school diploma, and hell if I knew where it was now. In college I had focused on football, going into one of those bullshit programs of study that would allow me maximum time on the field. Three years in and I was heading for the draft. At twenty-four, my life was engulfed by this career. Hell, I owed everything to my throwing arm, and if I ever found myself with an injury, I would be screwed. Without football, I would have nothing to fall back on, which tended to be a pitfall for most athletes. When we are at the top of the game, nothing else matters. Not school, sometimes not even the people in our former life. There was no thought to the what ifs, the thought that we might not play professionally long enough to build up a fat bank account and a comfortable lifestyle for the rest of our lives. I know I hadn't, which was why this job was so important to me.

If I didn't climb the ladder back to the starting quarterback position, I could find myself traded again or worse, forced to travel overseas to play for a fraction of what I was making now.

Shrugging off my insecurities for the moment, I looked closer at the name on the certificates, wanting to put a name to her banging ass. She was still too preoccupied with her task to realize anyone else was in the room.

A frown crossed my face as I read her first name. I squinted. It was a distance away but my eyesight was perfect. *Lucia*. Surely not? The fucking therapist was Madam X? I looked back up at the woman who had yet to see me, her hair starting to tumble out of the neat bun at the base of her neck. My hands itched to curve around her ass, slide up her skirt and find out what was underneath. If this truly was the Lucia from the black book, then I had a perfect opportunity here. But the therapist? God, I couldn't have any harder job in front of me. No wonder Terrence and Trey weren't worried about their end of the bargain. I was as good as two grand down at that moment.

Pushing away from the doorframe, I started to move forward ready to turn on the charm, but my sleeve caught on the door's handle, and I stumbled into the office instead.

I looked up in time to see her jerk around at the sound, the chair wobbling precariously as she flailed her arms about.

With a burst of speed, I regained my balance and reached her before she hit the ground, her delicious body landing in my outstretched arms with a soft thud. I balanced myself under her added weight, wrapping my arms around her trim waist as she steadied herself against me. A flashback of how my gym bunny had ended up in my arms last night hit me. Hell, I must be starting a trend, gorgeous women falling into my arms at the weirdest moments.

Her eyes rose to meet mine and I was momentarily frozen by the familiar warm caramel color peering back at me, reminding me of a particular whiskey I often enjoyed. Then a bucket of cold realization doused me, my breath seizing in my chest. It was her, the woman from the gym that had left me horny as hell. I had found her. *Oh shit… I had found her!*

No fucking way. The woman in my arms was the same woman that I'd been trying to track down, Lucia and my gym bunny. And fuck, on top of that she was the therapist. I wasn't sure if lady luck was smiling down on me or laughing at me. Damn. Still, as the moment lingered, her still in my arms, her body felt so good next to mine. Damn near perfect.

"Um, Mr. Maddox, can you release me now?"

Still holding onto her tightly, startled by her words, I released her abruptly and caused her to stumble once more. My hand shot out and I grabbed her arm, feeling the softness of her skin under my fingers as I steadied her once again. She was wearing a sleeveless blue shirt to match the tight skirt, the material silky and clinging to her skin in all the right places.

Her face flushed and she immediately pulled away from my touch, straightening as she looked at me. "You're late."

"I'm never on time," I responded, taking in her features with both dread and excitement. Shit. Of all people, I was not expecting this. Not in my wildest dreams did I expect Lucia from the playbook to be the therapist. No wonder she was marked untouchable. If Lucia's credentials were real—and from the display of certificates on her wall, they were—she could read anyone like a book, making it extremely difficult to pull one over on her. But hell, she was a great kisser. One I had fucking dreamed about.

A frown appeared on her face, and she cleared her throat. "Well, Mr. Maddox, I expect all of my patients to be on time. My calendar is very important to me, and I like to stay on track."

"Maybe you shouldn't have the meetings so early in the morning," I grumbled.

She pursed her lips and pointed to the chair in front of her desk. "It is not my fault that you chose to be out late last night… getting up to no good. Sit. We are already behind."

Chapter Six
LUCIA

He was here. I couldn't believe that he was taking a seat in front of my desk, though the surly expression on his face told me this was the last place he would like to be.

Feeling somewhat disoriented myself, I made a great show of placing my shoes back on my feet and sliding my chair back to my desk, wishing that he had not seen me standing on it and nearly falling flat on my face. Surely he had had a good view of my backside for a few moments, though I didn't know exactly how long he had been standing there. The thought both unnerved me and excited me. I could still feel the weight of his arms around my middle, the smell of him assaulting my senses and sending my body into overdrive. After the kiss last night, I had gone home to my pitiful TV dinner, but my thoughts had strayed to that kiss more than once. My dreams had been filled with it. Was I so pathetic that one kiss, one searing kiss, could take over my thoughts so much? Or was it more pathetic that I craved his touch again?

I looked up to find him watching me intently, and I instantly blushed. Glancing back down, I fidgeted with my notepad and pen. I knew I shouldn't be thinking that way with him right in front of me! I was a professional, with a client in the room, and all I could think was how nice his arms had felt around me. Like they belonged there.

"So do we just stare at each other or what?"

I cleared my throat and pulled out a file, already labeled with his name in bold print.

"Of course not, Mr. Maddox, it won't be that easy. I am Lucia, the team's performance therapist. Performance therapy is a relatively new field, so if you're not familiar with how this works—I don't believe your previous team employed one—I will go over a few of the basics, okay?"

"Fine by me if we can be quick."

His desire to leave made me bristle, and I sat up in my chair, urging myself to make stern eye contact. "I will be scheduling times with you to find out how you are with a number of things, namely how you are fitting in with the team and if you are experiencing any issues. And just so you are aware we do not condone bullying of any kind, hazing, or discrimination, so if you or anyone on your team is caught doing so, there will be consequences for your actions."

"Did I just step back into high school?" he teased, his blue eyes twinkling with laughter.

I gave him my best no-bullshit look, hating the way he made me feel—like I should be stripping off my clothes before him. His teasing nature could rattle anyone, pulling them off-track, but I was going to show him that I was not so easily flustered. At least that's what I told myself. "This is a serious matter, Mr. Maddox, and I expect you to treat it as such."

"Sure," he replied, leaning back in the chair. "Go ahead, Doc, therapy me away."

I fought the urge to throw something at his cocky smile. "We'll start small. Is there anything you would like to discuss? Are you anxious after your move?"

"Am I really here to discuss my feelings?" he asked with a sharp laugh. "Well, fine, today I am feeling like shit, Doc. Don't suppose you have an aspirin, do you?"

"That's not what this is about," I said tightly, hating those that didn't take this seriously. I had come onboard to make a difference in their lives, to provide them an outlet with someone open up to—anything that was driving them crazy and affecting them on the field. Most of the players were under a great deal of stress, trying to balance work and their home life under intense pressure and scrutiny. I wanted to be there to listen and offer advice, to give them the resources they needed to be successful, and most importantly help them succeed and focus when it mattered during games.

But most of them didn't give me a chance to offer even the slightest bit of advice. Most of my time was spent trying to coax even one word out of them. Clearing my throat, I regarded another jokester in front of me. "I am sorry you are feeling bad. Perhaps you shouldn't drink so much."

"Fair point," he grinned. "But it was fun, wasn't it? Do you ever have any fun, Doc?"

"We aren't here to talk about me," I replied, folding my hands on the desk. I wasn't going to comment aloud, but last night, for a brief moment, I had experienced a taste of fun. I just hated the fact that it had been with him.

"And I don't want to talk about me," he said, rubbing his hand over his hair idly.

"This is a complete waste of time. I could be out training right now, not talking about my childhood and shit."

My ears perked up and I leaned forward. "You would like to talk about your childhood?"

His face grew pale and he immediately shook his head. "Hell no, I don't want to talk about my childhood. I'm done."

I watched as he rose from the chair and started to leave, and panic started to set in; I was about to lose another one—Coach Hanshield will be pleased, I thought. I couldn't let him go! I had yet to keep any player in the seat for longer than five minutes since I had started, and if another one walked out without scheduling a routine appointment, I was going to be in trouble. I needed one success story. I needed to prove that this really worked, that I could make a difference!

"No, wait, please," I started, standing. He stopped and looked back at me, some of the color returning to his face. Obviously, his childhood was a sore subject. I would make a note of that later. "I'm sorry. I can help you however you would like. We can talk about anything or nothing at all, just please, don't leave."

He looked at me, and I knew I sounded desperate. I *was* desperate. This whole thing

needed to work, otherwise I might as well pack
up my diplomas and leave with my tail firmly
between my legs and with the shame of letting
my father down hanging around my neck. I
already lacked the confidence of the majority
of the coaches, and if my father got wind that
I wasn't having any success with the rest of the
guys, I knew that would be the end of this little
experiment. After all, my father wasn't known
for wasting money. I would be a failure, the one
word I could not stomach. I was more than that.

"Why?"

"I... er, because." How could I find the words
to explain it all to him, to open myself up to that
kind of scrutiny? This wasn't my therapy session,
for God's sake.

"You really need for me to do this, don't you?"

I cringed at the way he said it. I should just let
him go, wallow in my self-pity, and move on. "I
do," I all but whispered, feeling a bit useless. "I
really need this to work."

A strange look crossed his face as he walked
back toward the desk, his intense eyes staring
into mine. "OK, fine. But on one condition."

"What is it?" I asked, breathless with anticipation.
Short of sleeping with him, I would do anything
to keep him here.

He grinned then. "A date."

"What?" I responded, surprised. A date? No I couldn't go on a date with him! I had a strict no-player policy built into my contract. Besides, my father would kill me if he found out. "No I couldn't possibly. It's not allowed."

"Oh well, then I can't come visit you regularly," he replied with a sad, exaggerated shrug. He was loving this. "Sorry, Doc, those are my terms."

"One date?" I asked hesitantly. It wasn't that I didn't want to go out with him. He was after all Jacob Maddox, handsome, cocky, and could kiss like the world was ending. I could only imagine what type of date we would have, but I had to stick to my guns, right? If I gave in just one time, I would be treading into some dangerous waters in more ways than one.

"One," he replied, holding up one lone finger. "But sometimes you can't just stop with one."

I sighed loudly and sat back in my chair, glancing at the calendar before me. Could I make this work? I had to didn't I?

"Fine, one date. I have an opening this Friday." That was two days from now, giving me plenty of time to prepare for him and whatever antics he might try during the date.

"I'm free after eight," he said, a grin appearing instantly on his face. I nodded and wrote down my address on a pink sticky note and handed it to him.

"Here, pick me up here."

"See you then," he said.

Before he could walk out the door, I quickly added, "There will be no kissing! Or... or touching!"

"Oh, Doc, I can't promise anything of the sort." He winked at me then started to whistle as he turned away.

I scrubbed my face with my hands and fought the urge to scream. What had I just done? I felt like I'd made a deal with the devil. Not only had I agreed to go out on a date with him, but he'd managed to wangle his way out of the therapy session we were having! I groaned. He'd played me. And I could lose my job over this—breaking my contract so openly—but if I didn't get him on my side, I was done for anyway. Just one massive leap of faith, and perhaps the outcome would be worth it.

Chapter Seven
JACOB

whistled as I walked out of Lucia's office, feeling smug. I had just talked the woman deemed unfuckable into a date, even if I did have to resort to messing with her head a little.

Though—and I wouldn't tell her—the desperation in her eyes had tugged on something deep inside me, reminding me of my own past. Lucia had some deep need to make her job work. And besides, I didn't know if I could've still walked out had she turned down my offer.

She had determination, and I could relate to that feeling. But she had also revealed a weakness to me, which I supposed had given me a leg up on the competition, and really, I had gotten what I wanted in the end. I was well on my way to winning two grand and had a date with a hot chick. I had fucking enjoyed her kiss the night before, and I wanted more, a lot more. She was coy, though, I had to give her that. No wonder she had looked at me so oddly last night when I'd asked her about Lucia. She was Lucia. I still was struggling to grasp that concept. Yet looking down at the paper with her address and cell number on it, it didn't matter anymore, and I couldn't help but grin.

I walked to the locker room, where some of the guys had already gathered for the day's late-morning practice session. It was the last thing I wanted to do with my head still buzzing, but I had no choice. A downside of the job, having to go out into the heat with a fucking hangover. At least in Minnesota I had a fifty-fifty chance of having some cool weather to practice in.

"Jacob, my man! How did you like the party last night? Wasn't it everything I said it would be?"

I looked over to see Terrence coming toward me, the ever-present toothy grin on his face. "It was, it was! And actually it was exactly what I needed."

"You sure are in a good mood. Hell, I have a hangover to end all hangovers. But I can't wait to find out, did you find her?" Terrence asked as he threw his bag into his locker, the sound making us both wince.

"When you left last night you were so determined."

"Oh, I found her, all right," I said with an eager grin, glad that I could at least give him that information. "And I got digits and a date."

Terrence's smile slid sideways, his eyes rounding slightly. "You're fucking with me, right? I know you are. There is no possible way you could have gotten that far in one night."

I shook my head and held up the piece of paper, not showing him the info. I didn't need him encroaching on what I considered my territory. I was going to tame Lucia and enjoy every minute of it.

"Shit, man," Terrence said, eyeing the note, apparently trusting me as a man of my word. "How did you do that?"

"Charm, my man, charm," I laughed, placing it back into my pocket for safekeeping. "Why didn't you tell me she was the performance therapist? I would have prepared myself before she started picking my brain apart."

"Oh, you know," Terrence drawled as he pulled on his pads, "that would've been too easy. Besides, if we had told you, would you still have gone after her?"

I thought about that for a moment, thinking of how the lull of her missing identity made it all the more intriguing. Just the missing link had been enough to push me. "Nah, probably not."

"Well," Terrence said as I pulled on my own pads and laced my cleats. "You won, dude. No need to go through with the date now. It's all over." When I didn't respond, he leaned up against the locker with his forearm. "Wait. You aren't seriously considering going through it, right?"

"Why the hell not? I still need to get her into my bed," I shrugged, slapping him on the back for good measure. I had worked this hard to find out who she was, and that kiss, the one that Terrence didn't know about, was still on my mind. If she had blown me away with just a kiss, I could only imagine how it would be to get under the sheets with her. Under that prim and professional look of hers, I was betting on her being a wild ride. She just needed the right guy to bring it out of her, and I wanted to be that man. She was a conquest now, like a game I was told I couldn't win. There was no way in hell I was going to back down at this stage.

"Shit man," Terrence said as we started to walk toward the exit. "If you do this, you might not come back out. She will have you spouting that therapy crap before the end of the season, and then you can kiss a starting position goodbye. Ain't nobody gonna survive when her fa—"

"Stop worrying. Have more faith in me than that, Terrence," I interrupted, shielding my eyes as we stepped out into the sunshine. By the end of the season, I planned to have her in my bed and out of my system, and I'd be in that starting position. It was a good play.

Chapter Eight
LUCIA

I looked at the dress with a critical eye, turning it a few ways before throwing it onto the growing pile on my bed. For the last hour I'd attempted to find something to wear for the date, going through most of my closet before coming to the conclusion that one, I had nothing remotely sexy in it, and two, I needed to shop more. My clothes were either professional or comfortable. There was no in-between. I finally decided that it showed how unbelievably pathetic my life was.

With a grimace, I picked up my first choice, a strappy sundress that was many years out of fashion; it fell just above my knees and showed off the arms I had been working so hard on in the gym. The color was perfect for the hot weather, even if I thought it was a bit too revealing. I slid it on and left my hair down, taking a look in the mirror once more. I hated it—I looked fake, like I was trying too hard or as if I were attempting to slip on another personality—it just wasn't me... but it would have to do.

There was a reason I had such a pitiful wardrobe, and it all had to do with the fact that I felt comfortable dressing professionally. I was taken seriously most of the time in a good suit; it was a badge of security in a world that was dominated by men, especially in the football industry. In my suits and pencil skirts, I felt like I belonged amongst them. But in something like this, they would see me as an object meant to be seen and not heard. I couldn't stand that. I had worked and studied too hard to be seen as a floozy with a great rack.

Turning away from the mirror, I put my hand on my stomach, feeling the worry starting to knot up again. The thought of calling to cancel crossed my mind for the billionth time that day. I had a great deal on the line, and if anyone found out that I was out with a player socially, I would lose all credibility amongst the staff. The entire organization, for that matter. But the thought, the small thought, that if I did this that it would turn my career around still loomed in the back of my mind. Those damn 'what ifs'. They always made people do stupid things.

I walked into the open plan kitchen, hunting for a cracker to nibble on so I could calm my jumbled nerves. The guest house was fifteen hundred square feet, more like a regular-sized house. It had three bedrooms with adjoining baths, much too big for one person. But the rent was free, and when one only needed a place to crash at the end of the day, it worked out just fine. Plus it kept me close to my family, close to the people who knew me best. It was safe and uncomplicated.

I opened a cabinet and frowned, seeing nothing peering back at me. Damn. When was the last time I had bought groceries anyway? The clock over the stove told me I still had about an hour before Jacob was due to pick me up, which admittedly wasn't the best plan in the world. But I planned to be waiting right outside the driveway to bar any reason for him to come up the drive and knock on the door. The last thing I needed was him to cause a stir with my father. He for one could not know that I was going out with a player tonight.

All of my life I had been around football; my father's love of the sport made sure of that. When he had made enough money from his very successful brokerage firm, my father had jumped at the chance at buying a local team, haggling out a price to keep them right here in Jupiter. I could still remember the day that he looked at me and told me the news, how we were going to create and leave a legacy. "Everyone will know our name, Lucia," he had said as we stood in the owner's suite overlooking the field. "I will stock this place with such fine talent that no one will ever question my existence." And he had. My father had brought in more players with unquestionable ability in the last ten years than any other football team in the nation. And most of them came from our home state—home-grown—which made it all the sweeter, not to mention the stadium was almost always packed.

My stomach rumbled again and I slipped on a pair of sandals, grabbing my purse just in case I did not make it back to the guest house in time. The main kitchen was always stocked well, so I knew I could find something to eat in there and hopefully not run into my father. Normally in the early evenings he was poring over the books or going over films of potential prospects in some conference room with the rest of his operations staff. While some team owners had no buy-in other than making money, my father was always heavily involved in the minutia of the team.

I closed the door behind me and followed the path by the pool to the main house, and entered through the back door that led to the kitchen. The house was quiet, the housekeeper gone for the day, and as I walked into the large kitchen that looked like it had been pulled out of one of those food magazines, I breathed a sigh of relief that my father was not there.

Merry, my stepmother, sat at the granite island, a cup of coffee beside her as she looked over a stack of thick papers and folders before her. Merry was my dad's second wife. He married her a few years after my mother died of cancer. I was three when Mom died, and I vaguely remembered her leaning over me, the smell of her crisp citrusy perfume enveloping me as she picked me up with a smile. My dad never talked about her, and I suspected he was devastated when she died. But he was lucky to find love again. He and Merry got married when I was ten, and I was very fortunate that she loved me just like I was her very own child. No evil stepmother for me, I thought with a smile as I gave her a quick hug. I had a close bond with her, and she had always been my cheerleader throughout all of my education.

"Hey, sweetie," she said as our embrace ended. "You look pretty tonight. Got a hot date?"

"I do, actually," I laughed as I leaned against the island. "Do you have any crackers?"

"I think we do," Merry replied, pursing her lips. "If not, there's some leftover spaghetti in the fridge. I cooked it last night."

"That's too heavy," I said, walking over to the cabinet and starting my hunt. "I don't even know if I can keep these down." Finding what I was looking for, I grabbed a bottle of water out of the fridge and joined her at the island, the smell of coffee wafting through the air. "So, what's up?"

"Shouldn't I be asking you that? I want to hear all about this mystery date."

"Maybe later," I replied as I took a sip of the water.

"Fine, be all secretive. Anyway, I'm thinking about remodeling the den," Merry frowned, revealing that the stack of papers were sketches. "I'm getting that itch, you know?"

I smiled, taking a bite of a cracker, knowing full well that Merry couldn't stop remodeling the house. She had been an interior designer before marrying my father, which by happenstance was the way they had met all those years ago. I remembered the day we'd viewed this house, and Merry had been brought in to listen and observe in case there was something that my dad didn't like about it. It had definitely been a mutual attraction from the start, and they were married a year later. Since then, Merry had made it her personal mission to make the house exactly like they wanted it, which often resulted in grumblings from my dad about the cost and the mess. But he let her do it, regardless. "How many times does this make?" I teased, receiving a swat on the shoulder in return.

"Come on," she said as I took another cracker out of the box. "Tell me more about this date, I'm dying to know. It'll take my mind off all of these swatches. I'm so glad to see you are getting out of that guest house, Lucia. You work too hard, just like your dad. You need to go live a little. So, tell me, is it anyone we know?"

I shook my head, inwardly cringing at what she might think if she knew who the date was with. "No, he's just a friend from college." I hated lying to her. Merry was not only my stepmom, but also a very close friend for me, a confidant who knew just about everything about me and what went on in my life. And though I knew I could trust her, I held back, not wanting to see the disappointment in her eyes as she learned I was going out with a player. The guys on the team that weren't married had reputations for, well, being playboys. I was certain that Jacob was probably the same, but something in me craved that type of attention. It was wholly out of my comfort zone, and for once in my life, I wanted to be able to throw the caution to the wind so to speak.

"Well, I am sure he's fabulous," Merry continued, taking a sip of her coffee. "Where are you going? Is this just a dinner date?"

"What date?"

I closed my eyes briefly as I heard my father's voice echo behind me. I had hoped to escape this house without him knowing I was going out, but apparently he was back earlier than I had anticipated.

"Honey! You're home early! Just in time to help me choose a new color scheme for the den!" Merry exclaimed as my dad came over to kiss her affectionately. "And how was the meeting?"

"Horrible as usual, but we're making progress on the campaign. Tomorrow we're good to go," he responded, his gray eyes landing on me. "What's this I hear about a date, Lucia?"

"It's just dinner," I said casually, though inside my stomach was back in those tight and twisting knots again. "Nothing important."

My dad frowned, his bushy eyebrows knitted close together. "Do I know this fellow?"

I resisted the urge to bite my lip and shook my head, sticking to my original plan to keep this one a secret.

I had to. If my dad found out, I would be out of the organization faster than I could pack those diplomas back up. He never liked the idea of me being around the players when I was growing up, but I had always been treated with respect. No one was brave enough to ask me out. It was like they knew I was off limits. But here I was, going out on a limb, going behind my dad's back and having a date with a player. This was insane. Had I lost my ever-loving mind?

But the rewards were going to be so sweet if I went through with it. I could sense an issue with Jacob and his childhood in our initial interview, a trigger that had caused him to freak out and cover his discomfort with his charm. I couldn't help but wonder how long he had been doing that. Something in his childhood was not positive, and I wanted to tap into that aspect of his past so I could help him out. Perhaps it was even the cause of his troubles at his last team.

"Am I going to meet him? I believe I have the right to know who's taking my daughter out."

I sighed, bringing my thoughts back to my present issues. "No, Dad, that is so high school. I'm old enough to go out on a date without your approval."

"But it's my right as a father. I need to know they are good enough for my little girl," he shot back, his expression growing dark.

"I'm not so little anymore." I looked to Merry for help, and she winked at me before sliding her arm around my dad's waist. Her touch immediately softened his gaze, and I watched as he looped his arm around her waist in return. She had that effect on him.

"Now David, Lucia's a grown woman," she replied, squeezing his waist. "She knows how to pick out a good apple by now. I don't think she needs our help."

"Fine then," my dad replied, his expression telling me he didn't like it one bit and that the conversation was far from over. He would bring it up again and again until I told him. But with Merry's help he changed tactics. "How is the job going? Are you all settled into the new office? I'm sorry we had to move you from the main building, but I thought being closer to the players would help."

"I'm fine, Dad," I replied, giving him a small smile. "The office is perfect actually, it was a good idea being closer to them, and my calendar is starting to fill up." I didn't want to tell him that most of the appointments were with the clerical staff and not the players as I had hoped.

"Good, good," he said, stepping away from Merry. "You let me know if you have any issues okay, Princess?"

"I will, Dad," I said, my heart warming at the support that he was giving me. I was so lucky to have a dad like him, and yet I was betraying his trust. He would be so disappointed to know what I was about to do tonight. I had been a child who always followed his instructions to the letter, never giving him any worries as a parent when I was growing up. But this one date was going to totally destroy that relationship if he ever found out.

My purse started to vibrate beside me, and I opened it, pulling out my cell phone. It was an unfamiliar number, but in my gut I knew it was Jacob. He was calling to cancel. He had changed his mind and didn't want to be subjected to me or my therapy sessions. Realizing my parents were waiting for me to answer, I gave them an apologetic smile. "Sorry, I've got to take this," I said as I walked out of the kitchen and outside, where I would have some privacy. With a deep breath, I answered the call.

"Hello?"

Chapter Nine
JACOB

"**H**ey, gorgeous," I responded, hearing the hesitancy in her voice. She thought I was canceling our date. I could almost bet my bank account on it. "What are you doing?"

"I, um, I'm standing outside," she replied. "What are you doing?"

I grinned, thinking that she was horrible at small talk. Flustered by yours truly again. "I'm talking to you, of course." She let out a throaty laugh and I shifted in my seat, my cock springing to attention. Hell, I was ready to pop. "I've got a small issue that I hope you can help me out with."

"Is it truly a small issue or a big one?" she asked, a tease in her voice. I was momentarily taken aback by her banter, my grin growing wider. Maybe she wasn't that anxious after all.

"Well, you are going to have to wait and see," I said, my voice dropping down a notch as I walked out of the complex and towards the garage where my car was parked. "But seriously, I have been waiting to view this house on the waterway for days, and my realtor just called, saying that someone else is about to put a bid in. I need to go over there now to view it."

"Oh," she replied, the barest hint of disappointment in her voice. "Of course we can reschedule."

"I'm not asking to reschedule," I answered, climbing into my car and starting the engine. "I'm asking if you'd mind meeting me there instead? It would be an unconventional date, but I thought we could kill two birds with one stone."

"You want me to come with you?" she asked, surprise in her voice. I pulled the car out onto the highway and slid on my sunglasses to stave off the dropping sun. The house was a hot commodity, and as soon as I had seen it online, I knew I wanted it. Unfortunately, I wasn't the only one who did. So when my realtor called and said she had put me in a slot with a potential bid coming down the pipe, I jumped on it.

"Yes," I finally said, realizing she was waiting on my answer. "Come help me pick out this house. I could use another opinion, and I promise to throw in dinner afterward for the actual date."

"Um, okay," she said, uncertainty coating her words. "Text me the address. I can meet you there."

"I can't wait," I said before ending the call and sending her the address. There was no way in hell I was going to break this date. I had a bet to win and a woman to seduce.

I arrived a few moments later and pulled my car into the circular drive, noting the realtor was already standing on the steps. "Mr. Maddox," she said, extending her hand and broadening her already wide smile. "I am so glad you were able to view the house tonight, I know you must be very busy with the team, of course. I'm confident though the house will be everything you hoped for."

"Oh, I'm sure it will be," I replied, taking a look at the outside and releasing her hand before she got the wrong idea. The handshake had gone on too long, and like an eager puppy she was standing too close, hoping that I'd notice her. She would be out of luck tonight, I thought, I had a two-fold mission, and she wasn't part of the plan, though on any other occasion I would've taken full advantage of her not so subtle flirtations.

The house itself was two-story detached building, with a stucco exterior like all the others on the block. The tall iron fence that surrounded the property was a seller for me, providing that added layer of security, as well as the waterway in the back that I couldn't wait to view.

"Shall we go in?"

"I'm waiting on a friend to come."

"Certainly," the realtor replied, perhaps with a tinge of disappointment. Who am I kidding? Her face dropped visibly; she knew I wouldn't be banging her over the kitchen counter like I'm sure she'd fantasized about. "I'll head on inside and put the lights on. Come on in when you're ready."

I gave her a winning smile—the least I could do—and turned back to the driveway to watch Lucia pull in through the gates; her small four-door car stopped and parked behind mine. As she exited the car, I took in her long hair that brushed past her shoulders and then the slinky sundress, the hem that rose to her mid-thigh revealing her bronzed legs as she climbed out. Oh hell, she was hot. I couldn't deny the fact that I enjoyed her professional attire, reminding me of a naughty teacher, but in the dress that didn't disguise her curves she looked fucking fantastic.

"Hi," she said with a little wave as she climbed the steps to join me.

"Hey yourself, you look good enough to eat," I replied, struggling against my first impulse to push her against the column and have my way with her. She paused mid step and digested my flirty comment. "Thanks," she said softly.

"No, thank you for coming. I know this isn't what you had in mind tonight."

"Honestly I didn't know what to expect," she said as she looked around. "This is a big house."

"Big houses for big issues," I grinned, thinking of her banter earlier. She flushed and looked down, making me grin even more. "Come on, let's see the inside of this thing."

I allowed her to go in first, walking through the entrance into a foyer with tall ceilings and marble floors.

"Mr. Maddox, are you ready?"

I turned towards the waiting realtor and nodded, placing my hand on Lucia's lower back. She shivered lightly at my unexpected touch, and I applied more pressure with my fingers, wanting to slip lower onto that curved ass of hers. Hell, I wanted to touch her everywhere.

"This house has six bedrooms, with four full bathrooms," the realtor started, her voice a dull monotone. Her face had turned almost thunderous when she saw Lucia enter, but to Lucia's credit she didn't seem to have picked up on the realtor's hostility. She continued and pointed to a set of curved stairs to the left. "Upstairs there's also a game room, office, and the master suite."

I urged Lucia forward, and together we walked into the sunken living room, which crossed into the kitchen that was stocked with modern appliances. Granite countertops gleamed in the soft light, while stainless steel finishes twinkled. "The kitchen has been fully updated," the realtor explained, touching the cool stone surface. Lucia left my side picked up one of the brochures that had been placed on the counter and wandered over to the floor-length windows that overlooked the pool and waterway, her silhouette framed by the dying sun. I stood mesmerized, watching her take in the surroundings; she was to die for. The realtor droned on about all the amenities as I walked over to Lucia, looking at the manicured lawn. "The view… it's gorgeous," she breathed as the sun set over the water.

"It sure is," I said, looking at her. I could imagine her in that pool overlooking the waterway, the water sliding over her naked body. Just the thought made me want to buy the damn house. "Care to go upstairs?"

She turned towards me, her voice soft but her eyes sparkling. "Are you trying to get me into one of those bedrooms?"

I leaned in, not wanting the realtor to hear our business. "If I said yes, would you run the other way?"

She pursed her lips and I took in the heated look in her eyes, wondering about the last time the doc had been fucked, and I didn't just mean a quickie, I meant really fucked, ravished like she should be. So hard and so deep that it was almost primal. "You are being too forward, Mr. Maddox," she finally replied, looking away.

I tutted. "Jacob. You best call me Jacob if I'm going to let you see my future bedroom." I grinned, loving the way my words affected her. But not wanting to push her too far away, I altered my tactic. "Come on, Doc, you're safe with me." We walked away from the gorgeous view and were met by the realtor. "Would you like to see the upstairs now?" she asked, clasping her hands in front of her.

"I'm sure we can see to it ourselves," I replied, easing my hand into Lucia's. "We'll be right back."

"Um, sure—I will be here if you have any questions!" the realtor replied as I moved us both up the wide staircase to the second floor. The first bedroom we came to was the master suite, where I took in the spacious room, with only a stock bed in place. Beyond the walk-in closet and the master bath, there was a little balcony that overlooked the water, big enough for two lounge chairs.

"Now this is awesome," Lucia remarked as we walked out onto the balcony. "Imagine waking up to this view every morning."

"You don't live on the water?" I asked, wanting to delve just a little bit into her backstory. Beyond being the shrink, I didn't know anything else about her.

She shook her head with a chuckle, leaning against the railing to face me. "No, not really. I would love to but, oh, you are going to laugh at me."

I leaned up against the wall of the house, crossing my arms over my chest. "No, I won't."

"I live in my parents' guest house—the pool house," she said with a shy smile. "I know it's silly, but I've been in college like forever and just haven't found the time to go house-hunting yet."

"You can't have this one," I teased, drawing out another throaty laugh from her.

"No, I don't want one right now, I don't think. It's pretty nice to be able to walk over to my parents' kitchen when I want something to eat. And not have to worry about the upkeep."

"I can't disagree with that," I said, thinking that would be a sweet setup. "Are you an only child?"

She nodded, some of her smile fading. "I am. A daddy's girl, I'm afraid."

I maintained my smile, but inside I was cussing. Daddy's girls meant an overprotective male parent who would judge the fuck out of any man in his princess' life, therefore causing a living hell for the dating scene. But it also normally meant that the princess in question was just waiting to let loose, to break free of the innocent ties. All daddy's girls wanted to be wild little vixens when it came right down to it… they just didn't want to get caught. I could deal with that; there was nothing I liked more than the untapped potential of a sexually pent-up wild thing bouncing on the end of my cock.

"Is that a problem?"

I looked up to see Lucia staring at me, a smile playing around her lips.

"What? No, why would it be? I can handle you," I said with a sly wink.

"I imagine you could," she said softly, pushing

away from the railing. "So? Do you think you are going to buy this house?"

"Do you think I should?" I asked, really wanting her opinion. I knew nothing about buying a house; my last residence was a rented townhouse provided by my old team.

"I think it's a perfectly wonderful place," Lucia replied. "Maybe a bit big for just you? But the brochure says it has a good school district."

Laughing, I pushed away from the wall and followed her back into the bedroom to view the bathroom. I hoped I didn't have to worry about that for a good long while. Not that I didn't want kids one day—I did, just not yet. I still had plenty of wild oats that needed to be sowed.

The bathroom was just as impressive as the rest of the house, with a waterfall shower and a standalone tub that was positioned near the floor-to-ceiling windows. "Yeah, I think you should buy it just for the bathroom," she laughed, running her hand over the rim of the bathtub. "Screw the school district."

"If I do buy this house," I said, reaching out to cover her hand with mine. "Will you take a bath with me in that tub? I can't think of anything better than you all naked, wet and soapy."

She looked up and her lips parted, a breathy sigh

coming out of her mouth. "There you go again," she said with an amused but surprised shake of her head. I noted that she didn't exactly say no, though. One mark in the *she's fucking crazy for me* category.

"It's what I do best," I answered, my thumb caressing the top of her hand lightly, my body increasingly invading her space. I could feel her hot breath coming out in rapid waves—I almost had her, just needed to reel her in. "So Doc, what do you think? I'm dying to see what's under that dress of yours."

Chapter Ten
LUCIA

What did I think? What the fuck did I think? I was thinking all kinds of crazy, convoluted things about him, his innuendos, and his blatant suggestions. I was thinking about how wrong this all should be, but how right it really felt. I was thinking that I was torn between kissing him and running screaming in the other direction. I was thinking how fucking delicious the shock on his face would be if I let my sundress slip off my body and pool around my ankles in front of him. How good it would feel to get in that tub and let his hands run over my slippery body.

"I think," I started, swallowing hard, "there's no way we will both fit into that bathtub together."

His wolfish smile made me go weak in the knees as he leaned closer. "I would love to prove you wrong, Doc."

"Mr. Maddox, what do you think? Are you ready to sign on the dotted line tonight?"

I let out a pent-up breath as Jacob winked at me before turning around to address the realtor, who was hovering in the open doorway. "I think you have a deal. One condition, though. I want to move in immediately."

"I'm sure we can get you in by the end of the week," the realtor replied with a slight smile now, already pulling out her phone. "I'm sure the owners—"

Jacob shook his head, cutting her off with the wave of his hand. "No, I want in tonight or the deal's off."

I watched as the realtor's smile slipped just a little, unsure of herself for the first time. I knew that feeling; I was living that feeling right at that moment. "I, uh, that's an unusual request, Mr. Maddox."

Jacob narrowed his eyes. "Are you telling me it cannot be done?"

I felt sorry for the realtor, she paled, immediately shaking her head. "No, of course not. I just need your price, and I will make it happen. I promise."

EMILIA BEAUMONT

Her eyes flickered to me before she seemed to stand up straight again. She was jealous, it was pretty evident the moment I'd walked in the door, and she was perhaps thinking if she could get the deal done for Jacob that she would be in with a chance with him. But for some reason, which baffled and pleased me all at the same time, he'd barely paid her any attention... his eyes followed me instead.

I tried to hide my surprise as Jacob quoted a price, thinking of how much money he was about to put down for this house. For one person. It was insane.

The realtor disappeared through the doorway once more and Jacob turned his attention back towards me. "What?"

I shook my head. "You were a bit forceful with her about moving in here tonight. What's the rush? There isn't even any furniture in the place."

His grin slid back in place as he leaned in, reaching out to touch my cheek lightly. "See? That's where you are wrong. There's a bed. What else do I need? Besides, I always get what I want, so why wait?"

I swallowed hard, thinking about that bed. There was no doubt in my mind that he wanted to sleep with me. The question was, was I willing to sleep with him? I wasn't normally a casual fling kind of girl, but the need to have his hands on my bare skin was very evident to my poor, deprived body.

Just then my stomach growled, causing him to take a step back and breaking the potentially hot moment. "I'm sorry," I apologized, giving him a slight smile but feeling relief immediately. He was too close; I was starting to border on crazy notions that I shouldn't even entertain. It was like the closer he was to me, the more my rational thought just picked up its bags and moved away. "I haven't eaten properly since lunch."

He chuckled and tucked his hands in his pockets—perhaps resisting temptation to touch me again. "No, I'm sorry I haven't fed you yet. I promised you a date, a dinner date, and here I am buying houses while you're going hungry." Jacob looked around the bathroom with a critical eye. "How about we have dinner here? We can celebrate, plus I haven't explored the rest of the house yet, so we can poke around a bit, too. And I swear we'll get something better than takeout pizza."

My cheeks heated at the thought of him 'poking around' and I shook my head to clear the remnant dirty thoughts. The tub, the bed—they were still too close for comfort, and I thought I was in danger of stripping naked for him right there if we didn't go back downstairs quick.

It was a similar feeling you experience when you're at a great height, on a high bridge or a huge cliff, staring over the railing into a world of nothingness. And there's a small, insane voice inside your head telling you to jump, to let go— to fly... *to get naked.*

"No, I don't mind, but don't you think you're being a bit premature with the celebrating? The owners haven't even said yes yet," I finally replied.

"Oh, they will... and so will you. I'll get you in that tub one day."

Really now?

We left the bedroom, heading towards the staircase. He was excited about the house, and I was intrigued to see how the rest of this *date* was going to go—was I going to lose my mind? Or would I come out of it unscathed? I wasn't too sure which option I preferred. Either way, I was starving...

His smile told me I had pleased him with my earlier answer to stay and have dinner with him, and we walked down the stairs, finding the realtor at the bottom with perhaps the biggest smile of the night on her face. "I got it all set up, Mr. Maddox," she said breathlessly, her eyes sparkling. "The house is yours, and the owners have nothing against you, um, staying the night if you want. All they ask is a couple of season tickets in exchange."

"Done." He shot me a "told you so" look and I rolled my eyes at him.

"Good, I can bring the paperwork in the morning, and we can make it all official."

"That would be awesome," Jacob replied, giving the woman a grin. "Nine, then?"

"Of course. Good night and congratulations," she said, giving me another scornful once-over before handing over the keys to Jacob and hurrying for the exit. The front door shut behind her, and Jacob turned to me. We stared at each other in silence. The house was quiet with only my thunderous heartbeat as an accompaniment. I wanted to kiss him again...

Thankfully Jacob spoke up, breaking the spell and raising his phone in his hand. "I've got the perfect idea. While I order food, why don't you see if that pool is heated?"

"In Florida, everything is heated," I replied before the meaning of my words sank in. His eyes darkened, and I stepped back hastily, a little scared that he might jump me right there. Without thinking, I turned quickly toward the hallway. I hadn't been lying either, the thought surprising me just a little bit more. I was heated, desperately burning up more with each passing moment in his presence.

The humidity of the night air caused my dress to cling to my skin as droplets of sweat started to dot me all over. That was the only thing I disliked about Florida. The humidity made my hair frizz and my body always seemed to turn into a mini furnace. That plus the heat could be very misleading, and I wondered how Jacob was faring in the sudden change of climate from his previous team.

The patio was nice and spacious, complete with an outdoor fireplace area with grill and a bar— perfect for entertaining on the warm nights. I couldn't help but wonder why Jacob wanted such a big house when he would be the only occupant. My therapist's hunch was that he was trying to make up for something missing from his past, something that had a significant impact on his life. My other side stated that it was because he needed to show off. Either one was a possibility.

Stepping off the patio, I followed the small pebbled path to the pool, taking in the separate area that looked suspiciously like a hot tub, the colored lights under the watery surface glowing in the darkness. It was a pretty sweet setup, a house that I wouldn't mind having, but on a smaller scale. I knelt down and touched my fingers to the water, letting them trail and float on the surface. The water was definitely warm, but I couldn't decipher whether it was from the blazing sun or an actual temperature setting. Still, it felt right nice, and I found myself wanting to take a dip.

Though my father's estate had a pool, I rarely had time to use it lately. Too caught up with my work to take time out to enjoy the little things in life. Had I really become so tied up with my career that I had just weeded out the simple pleasures in life? How pathetic was that, anyway? Maybe it would be wise to scale back a tiny bit, add a few non-work-related activities back into my day-to-day, and then I wouldn't be throwing myself at new players...

With a sigh I stood and shook out my dress to rid it of the wrinkles that had formed. I should leave. I wasn't stupid. I had a great deal on the line with what I was doing with Jacob. My personal rules, concern about losing my credibility, not to mention my own psyche, for that matter. I was taking a huge risk by allowing this to go beyond a silly dinner—because deep down I knew if I stayed, there would be more on the menu tonight than just food. But what if, in my sex-deprived state, I was reading too much into his flirtations? After all, just because a man said nice things to you, that didn't automatically mean they wanted to see you naked. What if he didn't want to sleep with me?

I laughed then. Who was I kidding? I remembered his earlier words, though—he definitely wanted to see what was under my dress and had even said as much. The question was, what was I going to do about it?

Chapter Eleven
JACOB

I opened the cupboard in the kitchen, whistling lightly as I found a box of candles that had been left behind by the owners. I had my house. Though the price had been steep, I knew the moment I walked into this place that I wanted it. And as long as I didn't get a career-ending injury or traded again, I wasn't going to regret the purchase, either. It had all the right elements, like the beautiful view of the waterway. It was spacious and was fitted with modern conveniences. The landscaping and amenities outside, which Lucia was currently checking out, were added bonuses.

Pulling the box down from the top shelf, I was glad to see that it also contained a lighter. Good.

I couldn't conjure fire out of my ass. I set the box on the counter and looked at my watch. The food delivery was going to arrive in a few minutes, and I planned to turn on the Jacob Maddox charm. Not quite knowing what she liked, I'd ordered a little bit from every cuisine I could think of. We would feast on the food, and if everything went to plan, I would end the night feasting on her.

What woman wouldn't melt over a nice dinner by candlelight under the stars? It was the stuff of those sappy romance novels, and I was about to blow this bet out of the water. I would be a very happy camper, and I wagered she would be, as well. Either way, neither of us was getting a raw deal.

From my vantage point, I could see Lucia standing by the pool, her arms wrapped around her waist as she looked out over the waterway. Despite having an ulterior agenda, I was enjoying her company. She was a witty, beautiful woman who was both intriguing and able to carry herself professionally. To me, that was a fucking major turn on. Playing professional football tended to lend itself to the same groupie issues that musicians faced. Every night there were some women waiting around outside the locker room, parking lot, or outside a house looking for that one moment when we'd notice them and would change their lives forever. Or so they thought. Hell, most guys who weren't married (and a few who were) gladly made those women's dreams come true—if only for a night or two. It was the nature of the game, of our lives. But if we paid too much attention to one particular woman, then she started to get the wrong idea, hearing wedding bells and seeing dollar signs. If a woman was smart, she would attract a player in another way, like Lucia was able to do without even realizing it. That was when a man was truly sunk.

The doorbell rang, shaking me out of my reverie, and I walked down the hall to the front door, finding a young guy dressed in a waiter's outfit on the step. His eyes widened as I opened the door, recognition dawning on his acne-covered face. "Oh my God, you're Jacob Maddox."

"I am," I said as he handed me the receipt to sign with a shaking hand. "Did you bring everything I asked for?"

"I, uh, yeah," he replied, handing over the picnic basket loaded down with goodies before pulling a bag off his shoulder and handing it to me, as well. "Here's the food. Dude, are you really here to stay?"

"Yup," I said and gave him a hefty tip in return, which he pocketed immediately.

"Is this your pad?" he asked, looking up at the house in wonder. "Dude, it's sweet."

"It is as of tonight," I answered. "But don't tell anyone, okay?"

"Yeah, sure," he replied, giving me a thumbs-up. "Hey, thanks for the tip. If you need anything at all, Mr. Maddox, just call and ask for Ted. That's me. I will take care of it."

"Hey, thanks, Ted," I said, giving him a smile. I turned back into the house, knowing full well that after tonight I was going to have to keep the main gates closed. It would be too tempting for Ted not to tell a few friends where I lived. It was just the nature of the beast, being a familiar face. Unlike some athletes and movie stars, I knew that you had to stay relevant, and to do that, people need to know who you are. Privacy was an illusion in this business.

Walking through the hall and into the kitchen, I gathered my box of candles and walked outdoors, where the temperature had cooled off slightly since the sun had gone down. Lucia gave me a smile as she saw me. I set the basket, bulging bag, and the candles in the grass beside the pool. "What do you have there?" she asked, curiosity in her voice.

"Dinner by candlelight." I smiled as I started

placing the candles on the tiled edging next to the pool so I wouldn't set the damn grass on fire.

She kneeled on the grass with a hesitant smile on her face. I reached into the bag and brought out the blanket I had asked for, followed by a bottle of chilled wine off the restaurant's menu. Lucia moved back so I could spread out the blanket, lighting the candles one by one until we had a soft glow to add to the colored lights within the pool. "You really thought of everything, it seems."

"Money talks," I shrugged as I pulled out the carefully protected glasses from the basket, unwrapping them before pouring the wine and handing it to her. "Besides, I prefer the privacy of this type of dinner."

Back on the blanket she kicked off her sandals, arranging her legs so her dress still modestly covered her. I didn't plan on that being the case for too much longer. "I think it's nice," she finally said, making my chest swell. Hell, yeah, it was nice. It was going to win me a bet.

"Hope you're hungry?" I asked, pulling out the plastic containers still warm from the restaurant. "I think I probably got too much. I ordered one of everything on and off the menu."

She chuckled and took a swallow of her wine, looking at the small pile I was starting to make with the containers. "Jeez, you weren't exaggerating. Were *you* hungry?"

"Always," I admitted, setting them aside and pouring a glass of wine for myself before holding it up. "A toast, to new beginnings."

She pursed her lips and clinked glasses with me, taking another long sip of the wine. "May I ask you a question?"

I nodded, curious, and she ran her finger around the rim of her glass, her movements drawing my attention in more than one way. Was she always so precise and gentle with her touch, or did she ever get grabby and demanding? I wanted to find out.

"What's it like having to move where your job takes you? Don't you miss your family?"

I drained my glass and reached for the bottle. "You mean what's it like being traded?" I replied, skirting around the other half of her question.

"Well, I didn't want to say it like that," she laughed.

I chuckled, as well, leaning back on one elbow. "Honestly?"

"Of course. No point telling me if you're not going to be honest."

I nodded, mainly to myself. This was new

territory for me. I knew we were just talking casually, but this went a little deeper.

"It sucks. One minute you are flying high, thinking you are doing a good job, and the next moment you are being handed your box of shit and told to get out." Thank God I hadn't been like a lot of poor saps who'd settled in permanently before their first year was up. Though of course secretly I'd dreamed of staying a very long time. "There was always talk amongst the coaches and the players that no one, unless you are fucking superman, should settle down until they were sure to the best of their ability and knowledge that they were going to stay longer than a few seasons. I had been lucky, I guess. My house was a rental, and when I got my walking papers, I managed to get another player to take over my lease agreement. Not everyone was that *lucky* though."

"Ouch," she said. "I hate that I asked."

I shook my head, looking at my glass. "It's fine, really. Stings, but it's the nature of the game, you know?" I then looked up at her. "How long have you been around football?"

"All my life," she responded quickly. "I, ah, I mean I've liked it all my life."

"So how did you get into this job then?" I prodded, wanting to know a bit more about her.

It was a weird feeling, because usually I really didn't care to know anything about the woman I was going to fuck, but, well, Lucia was different.

She cleared her throat and glanced out over the water, a pensive look on her gorgeous face. "I just wanted to help people, you know? You guys are under a ton of stress and pressure, so I thought it would be good to have someone you could go to and unload anything you wanted to. Bit of a niche clientele, I admit."

"Anything?" I asked innocently, causing her to swing her gaze back to me. "I would be careful with your words, Doc."

She blushed in the candle light and took a healthy swallow of her wine. "You always bring out the worst in me."

The worst, huh? She hadn't seen anything yet. I took my chance and caressed the back of her free hand. "What about the restless heat that I bring out in you... the one you're unable to cool?" I leaned forward, my mouth close to her ear. "I'm going to bring much more than that out of you... I'm going to make you scream and think you died and went to heaven."

She made a choking sound in her throat, hastily setting her glass aside. "I, uh, I have to go to the bathroom."

"Lucia, come back… I'll behave," I lied. "We can just eat, I'll be good." I watched as she stood up and walked quickly to the house, her purse banging against her hip from the force of her steps. Hell. I hadn't meant for her to abandon me that early. Had I pushed her too far?

Running a hand through my hair, I swallowed the liquid in the glass, wishing I had something stronger, like a nice whiskey or bourbon. What if she didn't come back? Then I would have to chase her…

Chapter Twelve
LUCIA

I closed the door to the bathroom quickly, biting my lip as I popped the lock for good measure before sliding down the door onto the floor, the cool marble causing goosebumps to appear on my legs. No, no, I couldn't deal with him! I was messing with someone way out of my league, but damn it felt good to have someone so into me. I was actually enjoying his company, and not just because he was making me feel all kinds of weird emotions for the first time in a long, long time. My insides were quivering with want and need, my pulse pounding in my ears as Jacob's silky words ran through my mind over and over again.

He wanted me.

I could hear it in his voice, see it in his beautiful eyes.

So why was I hiding in the bathroom? It was Jacob Maddox, for God's sake, who had set up a candlelit dinner for me. Me. Not a model or some socialite, but Lucia, the therapist who was stepping out of her comfort zone. I was scared shitless, unsure of what to do or even what to say anymore.

Reaching into my purse, I pulled out my phone and scrolled through my contacts until I reached a familiar name, pressing the button to dial the number.

"Lucia?"

"Cara," I said in relief, glad that she had picked up on the first ring. "I need some help."

"Why? What's wrong?" she said instantly, her voice littered with concern. "Who do I need to kill?"

I couldn't help but smile as I heard her voice, loving my bestie, Cara. We had met in college, both taking the same classes with the same goal in mind. While I was focused on my career, Cara was the wild and crazy side of the friendship. But I loved her all the same. "No one. I just need some advice."

"Okay," she said. "Lay it on me."

"So there's this guy," I started, blowing out a breath.

"Is he obscenely hot?" she interrupted before I could get anything else out. "I mean, like the complete package?"

I thought about Jacob, his handsome features and hot body honed from all of this training. "Y-yes, he is the complete package. A little full of himself but…"

"Then whatever you are contemplating, you should do it, *now,* Lucia. Live a little!"

"But it's complicated," I protested, crossing my ankles together as I stretched out my legs. "There are other parts to this that are totally not good."

"Oh, come on, Lucia," Cara said with a sigh. "Don't try to talk yourself out of it. You always do this. When's the absolute last time you got laid?"

I thought back to the last guy and sighed. It had been quite a while since someone had made me feel *that way.*

"I am going to take your silence for a hell of a long time," Cara continued. "What's going to be the end result of throwing caution to the wind except a wild, awesome night?"

"I don't really know," I said, biting my lip once more. I hadn't really thought past the naughty innuendos that Jacob was throwing my way. He definitely wasn't the commitment type of guy.

"So what's holding you back?" she questioned. "What's keeping you from going and grabbing the man by the cock?"

I thought about my job, my position I had worked so hard to get to over the last few years. The thought of that no longer being part of my life made me extremely nervous. But there was a part of me that was clawing for attention. The woman inside that I barely acknowledge day-dreamed and fantasized about nights like this. So why was I still hesitating? What was the likelihood that the worst would happen? Had I really allowed my job to swallow me whole, preventing me from experiencing *life*?

"Thanks, Cara," I finally said, pushing myself off the floor.

"Anytime," she said before clicking off. I replaced my phone in my purse and took one look in the mirror before leaving the bathroom, my jaw set and determined. As I walked outside, I found Jacob standing near the pool, his hands in his pockets. He turned at the sound of my footfalls, a sheepish look on his face. "Hey, listen, I didn't mean to offend you. I was going to come see if you were okay but thought you needed some time—er, what are you doing?"

I reached up and grabbed the front of his shirt and saw the look of surprise cross his face as I leaned in. "Shut the hell up and kiss me, Jacob. Before I change my mind."

His eyes went from astonishment, to shock, to full-on desire before his lips crushed mine, a growl coming from one of us, I couldn't tell who. I wrenched his shirt into my grip as his tongue delved its way into my mouth. His hands were all over my back, seeking a button or a zipper to get my dress off.

"Take this off before I rip it to shreds," he demanded.

Before I could talk myself out of it I pulled back out of his kiss and his embrace, and my eyes locked on his. I pulled my dress over my head, hearing his swift intake of breath as he feasted on the lace-edged bra and panty set I'd put on earlier—never really thinking it would ever progress to this so quickly, but a girl had to be prepared.

"Shit," he breathed, already yanking on his shirt to pull it over his head. "You are fucking gorgeous, Lucia. I can't promise I won't tear those panties right off you, though."

"You won't have to."

I gave him a saucy grin, my heart hammering against my chest as I threw my dress on the ground and reached behind my back for my bra clasp.

The blush pink bra joined my dress on the ground, and I heard him growl as he saw my breasts fully exposed. An intense heat coiled itself from deep below my belly as his eyes roamed my skin. I hooked my thumbs into the elastic side of my panties and wiggled them down a tiny bit. Deviously, before I let him see me completely naked, I quickly walked past him and stepped into the pool with a pleasurable shiver as the warm water lapped up around my thighs. I sucked in a breath when the water lapped against my bare pussy, enjoying the sensation for a second before semi-diving into the water. Fully submerged, I kicked away from the edge of the pool and darted towards the center.

I heard splashes behind me when I came up for air and turned just in time to see a very naked Jacob beneath the surface of the rippling water, his strong legs kicking effortlessly to catch up to me.

His arms snaked around my body and pulled me against him roughly, his warm chest pressed against my bare back, his lips finding the sensitive skin right below my ear. "Where do you think you are going?" he growled, his hands exploring the round of my ass and squeezing gently. "You're mine now." A part of me wanted to prove him wrong, that I was nobody's but my own, and was almost tempted to swim away. But the part of me that was so incredibly hot for him had other plans. Up on my tiptoes, I was able to stay afloat but hooked my arms around his neck for extra stability. "Really, you think so? Prove it," I dared him.

His eyes flashed eagerly, and then it felt like he had a thousand pairs of hands caressing me all over. They came up to cup my breasts, fondling them as water splashed up between us. His touch was still gentle on my skin, and I moaned as he pinched my erect nipples, a pool of heat exploding between my legs that had nothing to do with the warm water. I could feel his erection pressed against my belly, and I wanted him inside me.

One of his hands drifted down to my stomach, caressing my skin there before delving lower. "Open," he whispered. This was insane, I kept saying in my head—a mini mantra that was on repeat—but regardless my thighs parted for him, and I wrapped my legs loosely around his. "Good girl." Stroking his way down, he slipped two thick fingers between my lips, eliciting a gasp from me as he pressed against the tight nub.

"How long has it been since you've been touched?" he asked, his finger swirling around my entrance. "Too long?"

I nodded, unable to speak, the pressure mounting.

His lips found the lobe of my ear, suckling gently as I closed my eyes, concentrating on his hands on my body. This was what I wanted. I wanted him, and I wasn't going to rest until I was sated. "I'm going to fuck you so much, it'll make up for everything you've missed." He plunged his digits into my waiting pussy, and I bit my lip as I let my head fall limply back into the water. I floated as he drove into me, deeper with every thrust of his fingers. I tried to hold on, to let it last longer, but my orgasm hit me like a brick wall, and I shuddered, whimpering as Jacob scooped me back up and held me against him.

"I'm not done with you yet," he said finally after the last tremor subsided. "I want more. Do you want more, Lucia?"

That was a silly question I thought. "I-I want much more," I breathed. He pressed a hard kiss against my neck and then released me, my legs wobbly as he grabbed my hand and led me over to the steps. Jacob sat on the edge of one, with his back against the rim of the pool. His erection protruded up from his well-formed body, nearly grazing the water's surface. He was big, and I felt my knees weaken again. "Come here," he said softly, his eyes coolly assessing my body, though the heated look in his eyes told me he wasn't going to wait too long for me to make up my mind.

Taking a deep breath, I straddled him. His hands rested upon the ledge of my hips, his fingers elongating to knead my ass. With the swift tilt of his head, Jacob took a nipple into his mouth, and I had to brace myself against his body to keep my balance. He sucked and licked, and I could feel the thudding of my heartbeat become ever faster. I lowered myself slowly, relishing each bump and caress of the head of his cock against my hot center. But even I couldn't stand to wait any longer. I took him inch by inch. Some of his cockiness had left his face, his own heart rate beneath my hand picking up a notch. I leaned down and brushed my lips over his. "What are you waiting for, Jacob? Fuck me," I whispered, feeling bold and horny as hell.

"Your wish is my command," he growled, his hands gripping my hips roughly. I lifted them and he groaned, his hips moving up to meet mine in a full thrust. For a moment we struggled to find the rhythm, but finally everything clicked, and I was riding his cock in perfect sync with his hard, relentless thrusts.

Neither of us censored ourselves, our groans were loud enough to wake the entire neighborhood. I felt like I was on fire, and he was the only person that could put me out. Our pace increased, the water lapping up frantically around us—our very own wave machine—as I slid up and down on his shaft. My insides quivered, and my toes curled from the multiple orgasms he was giving me. One after another, never stopping. He was a literal *fucking* machine.

Jacob's grip on my hips grew tighter, his pace becoming more and more hurried, and his grunts deepened. He caught my stare and returned it, never looking away as he stiffened then let out a bellow-like groan. I cried out, too, as the most intense orgasm of the evening hit me. It caused me to lose all sense; the world went dark as I rode the wave.

Jacob's arms flexed one more time, making sure he was deeper than ever before I collapsed against his wet chest, my breathing harsh to my own ears as reality battered at the door. *Oh fuck me, what had I done?*

I had just had sex in a pool with a player. And not just any player, but Jacob Maddox, my father's newly acquired asset. It went against everything I had ever set for myself. I was fucked, in more ways than one.

* * *

I woke up with a start, my eyes focusing lazily on my surroundings before I figured out where I was. The heavy arm over my body told me that no, last night's events hadn't been a very vivid dream or fantasy but were in actual fact very real.

I had slept with Jacob Maddox—fucking like bunnies—numerous times until I couldn't keep my eyes open anymore. It had been then that Jacob had tucked us both in the only piece of furniture in the house, and I had fallen into a dreamless sleep. Careful not to wake him, I looked over at my sleeping partner, a slight smile on my face. He looked harmless in his sleep but no less handsome, his mouth slightly parted as he slept on. He emitted an occasional soft snore as he dreamed.

In this light he looked more like the Jacob I had imagined him to be—the one that I was sure he tried to keep hidden beneath the surface. Instead of the cocky heartbreaker and playboy, here beside me was a gentle giant—the real Jacob. The one who was romantic as well as a devil in bed. Temptation flooded my body. All I wanted to do was let my head rest back upon the pillow and nestle my body up against his as we dozed the morning away. But that would be too easy. I sighed knowing that unfortunately, *we* couldn't be. I couldn't see him again. *I wouldn't.* I was a professional, for God's sake, and he was one of my clients! I had broken a sacred rule of my profession. I could only hope that events of last night would successfully get him out of my system. I would go back to not needing sex, not needing to be touched... fuck, who was I trying to kid?

With a sigh, I eased myself from under his arm and reluctantly climbed from the bed, finding my sundress under the pile of clothes strewn about the floor, glad that I'd had the foresight to pick up my clothes from outside when we'd darted into the house naked. My panties and bra were tangled up with his boxers in a pile on the cold marble floor.

I ignored the uncomfortable feeling that settled deep within my belly, my heart aching slightly. I dressed quickly and silently before taking one last long look at him in the bed. I was doing the right thing by escaping before the awkwardness of the morning could happen. Honestly, I didn't know what I would've even said to him, other than that we couldn't do it again. If I stayed, he would give me those eyes, turn up the wattage of his smile, and before I knew it I would be back in his bed again. No, this was the way, to leave without letting him dig his claws back into me... If my father found out, I would be up the creek without the paddle or the boat. He would be so disappointed, and I would lose all credibility with him, not to mention the repercussions that could be coming down the pipe if anyone else found out.

Turning my back to the bed, I grabbed my sandals and padded downstairs as quietly as I could to where my purse was sitting on the kitchen island, right where I'd left it. It was time to get back to reality. I quickly checked my phone, more out of habit than anything, not really expecting a message, but there in the little inbox was a violent flashing number telling me I'd missed several texts and calls… most all from my father. *Oh God, he can't know already, can he?* With my heart beating frantically, I swiped to read the urgent texts.

From David Cortes - 06:04 - Lucia, don't forget about this morning. Dad x

From David Cortes - 08:21 - You've missed the rehearsal. Where are you?!

From Merry Cortes - 08:36 - Sweetie, let me know you're okay… you didn't come home last night. Your father is about to lose his mind.

From David Cortes - 08:49 - I ASKED YOU FOR ONE THING, LUCIA!

I swallowed. *Shit.* I'd completely forgotten today was my dad's important day. With a quick glance at the time, I saw that I could still make it. But I wouldn't be able to go home and change. I would be stuck in last night's outfit that reeked of sex... and Jacob Maddox.

Chapter Thirteen
JACOB

The bright sun and a loud thud greeted me as I woke. The sound of a door closing? As I lazily blinked my eyes, the night before came flooding back. Lucia, riding me on the pool steps. Carrying her over my shoulder up to the bedroom, where we made full use of the standup stone shower in my new bathroom before breaking in the bed in the master bedroom. Hell, I didn't even know whose bed it was, but damn, I had fucked like a king and slept like a baby in it.

Looking over, I puzzled for a moment as I noted that her side of the bed was empty. Not a surprise, really, but I still felt a twinge of disappointment. She had been a bit skittish at first last night, but she had gradually warmed up, and hell…

she was quite a woman when she let her hair down. No doubt she'd switched back to being a timid mouse again and had scarpered before dawn. It was refreshing in a way. Normally any women that I allowed to grace my bed would attempt to stay come morning, clinging to me and the sheets, hoping we'd cuddle or that I'd make breakfast. Desperation wafted from them as they dreamed of a future together... yeah, fuck that. They'd be thrown out as quickly as I could get them dressed. But Lucia, leaving without word? Well, that was different.

Stretching, I climbed out of the bed naked and strode to the balcony, watching as the boats sailed the inter-coastal waterway just outside. This was the house I had wanted, and now it was mine, minus furniture. Maybe Lucia could help me in that regard, as well. Now I wouldn't be able to even look at the pool without picturing her there, bathed in the moonlight.

The grin still on my face, I walked back into the bedroom and ducked into the bathroom for a quick shower. Once done and toweled dry I picked up my only clothing, which was strewn all about the floor. As I pulled up my pants, a thought hit me. I had actually won the bet. That damn silly bet that I couldn't bed the most untouchable woman in the playbook. "Hot damn," I muttered, but the smile had slipped from my face. The bet sounded damn ridiculous now. The doc was sweet and beautiful, and I'd enjoyed every moment of her company—so why was I feeling like such an ass?

My antics weren't any worse than I'd done before… I was a self-proclaimed womanizer, using and then losing them. And yet a sinking feeling of remorse settled low within me. I thought about Lucia and how her face would fall if she ever found out that she'd been part of a stupid bet. *Shit.*

I would've still been attracted to her had we not bumped into each other that night at the stadium, though the bet was a reason for me to press the issue just a tad further. I couldn't let her find out about it. She would think that was the only reason I had slept with her, and hell, I suddenly realized I wanted a repeat performance with her even though I had won. My body craved her.

Shaking my head, I threw my shirt on and walked out of the bedroom. I had to get to the stadium and get through practice first. Then I would sort it all out.

After dressing I quickly locked up the house and climbed into the car, my thoughts still on Lucia. How was she going to react this morning?

Would she be embarrassed to see me, regretting our time together last night? Or would all of the naughty things we had done together run through her mind? Would she would struggle to keep her sanity the rest of the day as I would? Either way, I was about to find out.

I slowed the car as I approached the stadium, frowning slightly as I noted the vast number of reporters crowded around the main gate. What had happened? Surely not another high-profile player grab.

As I rounded the gate and slowed to a crawl, I saw that a large platform had been set up. The owner of my new home team stood behind a podium facing a swarm of reporters. I recognized the PR rep to his right, and there was a tall, striking blonde woman—late forties or early fifties I would've guessed—in a tight dress next to him, a winning smile on her face as she looked up at him.

From what I'd heard, David Cortes was a real go-getter who didn't take any bullshit. He had taken the team and turned it into a very successful franchise. The players respected him, but he didn't coddle anyone. As I sat in traffic waiting to turn into the gate, I did a double-take as I spotted Lucia on the other side of Mr. Cortes, an apprehensive smile on her face.

She looked drop-dead gorgeous, but were those the clothes she was wearing last night? The moment she'd taken off that dress I lost all memory of it, preferring to memorize the curves and sways of her body instead. But the vague recollection of her in yellow, a color that made her skin glow, was starting to come back to me. For hours I had licked and touched her body and watching her stand there, her hair a little bit mussed—far from the sleek bun I'd previously seen her with—she was starting to make my cock twitch. But what on earth was she doing up there? Had she won some award or something? If so, I couldn't wait to congratulate her in more ways than one.

Rolling down the window, I turned down the radio and listened as Mr. Cortes stepped up to the podium. Besides, traffic was at a standstill.

"Thank you all for coming today. This is a very special day for me and my family as we embark on a new adventure in all of our lives. I have given this very careful thought and feel it is time to put my stamp not only on our professional sports arena, but also on the political one. So, with my wife, Merry, and my daughter, Lucia, by my side, I am formally announcing my run for mayor of the great city of Jupiter."

My jaw dropped. I couldn't have heard right.

Daughter?! The rest of the world faded away, and I didn't hear anything past the announcement that Lucia was his daughter. Fuck me, I was going to hell in a hand-basket. My life was not going to be worth living... I had slept with the owner's daughter? For someone who was trying to make his mark and trying to become the starting quarterback again, that was the absolute shittiest thing I could have done.

Anger flared within me, and I gripped the steering wheel. Why hadn't she told me? Now all of her hesitations made sense—and here I thought she was just being shy. Hell, even her name in that book the other players kept hidden made a whole lot of sense! I was going to kill them. This was so far from hazing that it wasn't fucking funny. It was my livelihood, for fuck's sake... and perhaps hers, too, I considered. No wonder she was the untouchable woman. Hell, a man couldn't compete with her father, especially not one like me who would be staring his boss in the face when he found out that I had slept with his little girl! Dammit.

A horn blew behind me, and I looked away from the press conference, seeing that I was now the one blocking traffic and causing several people to turn and stare. With a growl, I threw the car into drive and gunned it through the gate, confusion and worry now coursing through my veins. I had slept with the damn owner's daughter. If I wasn't sacked by the end of the day I would count myself lucky.

It didn't take me long to park my car and walk into the training room, where some of the guys were already gathered. I eased up to my locker, slowly forcing myself to unclench my fists.

"Dude! Hey, you sick or something? You look like shit." I looked up to find Terrence next to me, a concerned look on his face.

"I fucked up."

"Aw, hell," Terrence said, leaning in. "If you smoked it, I can get you some clean piss for a nominal fee. Wouldn't be a problem."

"No, I didn't do that. Actually, in truth, *you* fucked up," I said angrily, throwing my bag into the locker, mad at myself, Lucia, and Terrence, who'd gotten me into this mess. Not only that, I was mad at life in general. I had just found an amazing woman, and she was the only one I could never ever go near… again. Not if I valued my career. I couldn't be more pissed about that. "I won the fucking bet, Terrence."

Terrence took a step backward, his eyes widening. Clearly he knew who Lucia was. "You what?"

"I said," I growled, doing everything I could not to slam him into the locker, "I won the damn bet. I slept with X last night. Or should I say, Lucia Cortes."

"Oh shit," he replied. "I don't believe it. Seriously? Shit, don't you know who she is?"

I wanted to say that I couldn't believe it, either, but not for the same reasons he was probably thinking. "I do now, you asshole! What the hell am I going to do? This is all your fault, Terrence."

Terrence shook his head, pulling down his cleats from the shelf. "I know, fuck. I'm sorry, dude. We never thought you'd be *successful!* Damn, I wouldn't want to be you if Cortes ever finds out. You will be on his shit list forever and never get any playing time. He might even trade you over this. Fathers are protective over their little girls, you know? I hope to hell you gave it to her good so she doesn't have a reason to complain about you."

"Tell me something I don't know." I sighed and leaned against the locker, finding it hard to believe that just a few hours ago everything was going so damn well. "There's no way I can go to those therapy or performance sessions or whatever they are fucking called now." I couldn't face her until I had all of this figured out. I didn't know what to say to Lucia or how to even approach this news I had just learned. It could potentially mess with my career, and that was the one thing I couldn't afford to go south.

"Just tell Coach," Terrence answered as the buzzer sounded, indicating that it was time to go out to the practice field. "He hates all that mumbo jumbo getting in the way, hates that it interferes with his schedule. He doesn't like his players going. He'll get you out of it. If you want to skip it, he's your man."

I nodded. It was a start. But I promised her: one date in exchange for going to the sessions. She was going to be pissed. But maybe a proper clean break, with no contact ever again was going to be the best way forward and out of this mess.

My lips in a thin line, I grabbed the rest of my stuff and jogged out with Terrence, finding Coach on the sideline. "Hey, Coach, can I talk to you for a moment?"

"Sure, Jacob," he replied, a friendly smile on his face. The man was a pure genius, a coach that I enjoyed working with. I couldn't wait to run his plays for real and not just in practice. "Actually, I've been meaning to catch you, but reception told me they couldn't get hold of you—apparently you have a shit-load of messages at the desk."

"Ah, okay. I changed my number, you see."

He bobbed his head. "Well, just remember I'm

not your messenger, so make sure you update the staff."

"Will do, Coach."

"So what did you want to talk to me about?"

I swallowed hard, hating that I was going to do this right now, but hell, I didn't know what else to do. I had to get my shit together and fast, especially now with the hole I'd dug for myself with my actions. "I can't go to that therapist anymore. She's messing with my head." I hoped that would be enough; I truly didn't want to have to go into detail or lie any more than I already had. That was my business.

"I fucking knew this would happen," Coach swore, catching me by surprise before clasping me on the shoulder. "Don't worry. I will take care of this, Jacob. Thank you for coming to me."

I nodded and jogged off, my entire existence in turmoil. I'd hoped there would be a wave of relief after telling the coach, and yet there wasn't even a fucking smidgen. Why did I feel like I had screwed Lucia over, and not in the way that I wanted to?

Chapter Fourteen
LUCIA

"I've had enough of you!"

I looked up from my papers to see Greg storm into my office, his face red with exertion. "Excuse me?"

"You," he said, wagging his finger in my face angrily. "You are screwing with my players' heads and I won't have it. Dammit, Lucia, I put up with a lot of shit from your father, but you are messing with the team and their money making potential, and I won't let you do that."

I folded my hands together and looked him square in the face, tired of his opinions of my work. After my night and rush to work this morning—getting the cold shoulder from my father—the last thing I wanted to do was deal with Greg as well. "I am doing my job, Greg. It's part of their contract."

"Well, not anymore," he exclaimed, his words giving me pause. I was the owner's daughter, but this man ran my father's team. If he pushed hard enough, I would be gone. There was no way my father was going to choose my side or my job over his coach's wishes, not this close to the start of the season. Blood was blood, but money and success talked in this organization, and while Greg was an asshole, he was making my father a bucketful of the green stuff. "I'm pulling all of the quarterbacks from this immediately. Don't make me go to your father about this, Lucia. You keep on and I will have the entire team pulled, and you will be out on your ass, you hear me?"

I took a sharp breath and bit my lip, as I picked up on the fact he had specifically mentioned quarterbacks. That would mean Jacob was included. Had Jacob said something to cause this sudden embargo? Had last night not been as spectacular as I thought it had? He wouldn't do this, would he?

Unanswerable questions whirled around in my head, enough to make me dizzy. But when I truly thought about it, I didn't really know him at all, did I? One night full of sex and barely any talk was not the way you got to know a person.

And perhaps this was his way of telling me he didn't want to see me, that he was embarrassed he had slept with me?

When I had left that morning, my body had ached deliciously, and my heart was doing its best to convince my brain that it wouldn't be all that bad if I were to date a football player after all. Our night together had been way more than I had imagined, his playfulness making me feel like someone special for the first time ever, like a woman who was truly coming into her own. I felt more confident and slightly more brazen when I was with him—it reminded me of my former, much younger self. *My true self?* Me at the age of fourteen, when I barely concentrated on schoolwork and my life was filled with fun and laughter. Being with Jacob, and even only for one night, had caused a huge crack to form in the rigid life I'd built for myself… and shining through now were the possibilities of what could be, if only I widened the break instead of spackling over it.

But now Greg was threatening my job once again, and I hated it. I felt my hackles rise in defense; I wanted to go to war with him instead of backing down. I hated him, and I wanted him out of my office before I threw something at his balding head and definitely got myself fired.

"Fine," I finally said, gritting my teeth as anger and frustration welled up inside. "I won't see the quarterbacks." Giving him this little victory was probably going to come back and bite me in the ass, but for now I had to give in. Besides, perhaps not seeing the quarterbacks—Jacob—would make it easier to see him again socially, I thought with a teenage-like pang. God, I couldn't get him out of my head. Yes, with him no longer my patient it could work… I would figure out the rest later. Maybe this was a blessing in disguise.

"Damn right you won't," Greg said as he started to walk out. "Don't forget, if I find out that you are messing with anyone else's heads, I will pull them, as well. Don't push me on this, Lucia. Stay the fuck away from my team. You have no jurisdiction here, just another woman whose daddy is handing her a career."

He then stormed out, leaving me sitting there behind my desk, tears threatening my eyes. I would not cry over this, I would not allow him to goad me into thinking I wasn't making a difference! My dad had not given me this job. I had earned it, rightly. The diplomas on the wall gave me the right to do this. But, if it came down to me and Greg, my father would side with Greg all day long—especially after this morning's debacle.

Turning up late, and in last night's clothing, to boot (which Merry and Dad had both noticed, though Merry was discreet enough not to say anything) hadn't won me any brownie points with my dad. I'd seen the disappointment on his face, and I never wanted to see that look ever again. I would make it up to him somehow, be the perfect daughter for his mayoral campaign efforts and not give him any grief. Because now not only did he have a team to worry about, he also had an election to win, as well, and if word got out that his daughter was a hussy, sleeping around with the players while 'pretending' to be a therapist, my entire family would be sunk. My father would be pissed off, and I would be in a world of trouble. My reputation, professional and personal, would be shattered. Once a floozy always a floozy in many people's eyes.

Standing, I shut the door to my office and pulled out my cell phone, locating Jacob's number. I needed to talk to him, to find out one way or another what he was thinking and if he'd said anything that would give any kind of indication that we were sleeping together. If he didn't want to see me again, fine, but I wanted to hear it from him and him only.

The phone rang a few times and the voicemail came on, but I wasn't sure exactly what to say.

"Um hey," I finally decided upon, feeling foolish. "This is Lucia. Give me a call back when you get this. We kinda need to talk." Hanging up, I sat the phone back on my desk and forced myself to calm down. Greg hadn't alluded to the fact that he knew about my little date with Jacob—surely if he had, he would've used that as a fool-proof piece of ammunition to get me fired. And so far no one had come in to spread the gossip. My secret was apparently safe for the moment, and I hoped it would stay that way, but something told me that I should enjoy the slight relief because a storm was coming.

* * *

I walked past the locker room, feeling drained from the day's events. I'd hoped to run into Jacob at some point during the day, but so far he had eluded me and not returned my phone call. The door opened and the object of my thoughts walked out, surrounded by three other guys from the team. Our eyes locked, and I felt the heat of desire rise into my cheeks, the memories of what we had done just hours ago still fresh in my mind.

"Hey, Doc," he said, his grin now cocky as I stood there at a loss for words. "Like what you see? Or perhaps you are here for my autograph?"

"Oh shit," another player murmured. "He did not just say that to *her*."

I heard the remark and knew I had to respond just like I normally would but it was hard not to take his nonchalance as a slight. Had last night meant nothing to him?

"No," I swallowed, trying to put on a brave face so that he would not see the hurt. Hurt was a sign of weakness, and I was *not* weak, I thought as I grit my teeth. I really wanted to knee him in the balls, but my father wouldn't be too happy with that scenario, either, if he heard his daughter was roughing up the players. Plus it would bring about too many questions that I wasn't prepared to answer. "All I see before me is a boy who wants to be a man and is failing miserably at it."

Jacob's eyes flared with surprise as he registered the insult, and I felt a small amount of satisfaction. He had made me think about him all day long, and I was annoyed that he was occupying my thoughts so much. For the longest time I had been on my own and just like that—after a silly night of fun—it had all turned sour. I was back in that vicious cycle of lust, where a member of the opposite sex could have this type of effect on me, wreaking havoc on my life. I hated it. I felt like I needed to make an appointment with myself to have my head examined!

Obviously last night had been a huge mistake… what the hell had I been thinking? Players were all the same, cocky, womanizing playboys, and I was just another notch on Jacob Maddox' bedpost. I wanted to groan at my stupidity.

"Are you going to let her get away with that?" the player next to him said, his eyes on me. I knew him, and as much as I wanted to say that I knew about his own issues, I couldn't. I needed to be a professional.

"Well, Doc, I don't know," Jacob finally responded, his grin restored. He was back to full confidence. "Would you like to find out? I'm free later if you want your very own *session* with me."

The bastard! He'd known—somehow—what it meant to me to go on that date with him in exchange for him turning up for his sessions with me. Now not only was he not going to be coming to them anymore, and he'd obviously said something to the coach, but he was also throwing it in my face! I wanted to yell and let loose the anger that was building, but if I did that I knew something bad and regrettable would tumble out of my uncensored mouth. Instead, I narrowed my eyes to let him know I was not at all happy with him and stormed away, ignoring the laughter that followed behind me. Let them think that Jacob had one-upped me. We had bigger problems than that.

It wasn't until I was in my car that I felt the first

tear escape from my eye, then another, much to my dismay. I hated crying, especially over some guy who was an idiot. *Fucking jocks, they were all the same.* But I had slept with that buffed-up fool and my career, everything I was attempting to do at this facility, was in jeopardy. What was I going to do?

My phone rang, startling me, and for a stupid moment of hope—yes, I was pathetic—I thought it might be Jacob, calling to apologize, wanting to talk, to explain his actions. But Cara's number was on the display and I sighed, thankful that at least I had someone I could still talk to and rely on. I answered and held the device up to my ear. "Hey, Cara."

"Hey, babe," she replied. "What's wrong? You've got that 'the world has gone to shit' tone."

"Oh, it has, but it's too much to talk about over the phone," I said, "I sure wish you were a lot closer so I could lay it on you. Needless to say, guys suck!"

"That they do," she said slowly, "but consider me your fairy godmother 'cause the funny thing is, I *am* here."

"Here, here?"

She laughed at my eagerness. "Yes, I got in just a little while ago and wanted to see if you want to meet me for drinks."

"Oh, you have no idea how much I want that," I said, wiping the tears from my eyes. A good bestie talk was exactly what I needed, and it totally helped when your bestie was a therapist, too.

"Just tell me where and I will be there," Cara was saying, her chipper voice making me feel tons better already. I gave her the address of a bar I'd overheard the players recommend one time and then ended the call, turning the key over to start the engine.

* * *

"Oh my God."

I ducked my head and took another sip of my drink. "I know, right? What am I going to do, Cara? I don't think I can go back to work now. He'll be around every damn corner, waiting to pounce on me and rub it in. And if he hasn't already, the rest of the players will know what we did, and God… I don't think I could stand the whispers and knowing looks."

Cara shook her head, her short bob swinging with the motion. "Geez, Lucia. You can really get yourself into some messes. What happened to your no-player rule? Though it's partially my fault, I told you to go for it. But in my defense, I didn't know he was a player."

"Yeah, well, you haven't met Jacob," I sighed, and signaled for another drink. We were in a bar a good ways from the stadium, a hole-in-the-wall place that was apparently known for its margaritas and eclectic atmosphere. The place was starting to fill up, and I just hoped that no one from the team decided to stop in, or I was going to really lose it.

Cara sat back and looked at me, with the same concerned expression she'd had the entire time I was telling her the long, convoluted story of the mess I was in. While I knew she wouldn't judge me whatsoever, she was going to give her two cents' worth anyway.

"Well, was it good?"

"Cara!" I blushed, my mind thinking of exactly how good it had been. I had lost all my inhibitions with Jacob. The outdoor sex had been something that I never foresaw myself doing, and yet with him it had been easy to let down those barriers.

"You don't even have to answer now," she said, grinning. "It's written all over your face. Damn, maybe I should date a player, as well."

"What am I going to do?" I asked, feeling miserable. "What if he tells everyone? My father will kill me, Cara, and I will lose my job."

"It's interesting that you bring that up, 'cause I

think I might be able to solve all your problems," she replied, a gleam in her eye.

"Really? Can you erase my memory of what happened, or better yet his?"

"Oh, honey, I'm sure you don't want to forget what happened. From the look on your face before, it seemed like it had been one of the best nights of your life?"

"Maybe," I said with a sheepish grin. "God, it was amazing… but I want to know, how are you supposedly going to fix this?"

"Well, I have decided that I am moving here, to Jupiter, and starting my own practice. And I want to know, would you like to join me? Be my partner?"

"Are you serious?" I asked, surprised. This was the last thing I was expecting her to say. "What happened to the practice in L.A.?" Cara had joined a psychiatry practice in California that centered primarily on marriage counseling and also children's services. I had thought she loved her job, and she was very good at what she did, but something had happened. I could see it in her eyes.

She shrugged, her expression growing dark for a moment. "There was this widower who was bringing his daughter in for treatment. We had a thing, but it fizzled out, so here I am."

I watched the range of emotions that played across her face, knowing that there was probably more to the story.

"You need to talk about it, hon?"

"No, I'm good, really. Just need a fresh start, you know."

I nodded. She would tell me when she was ready and in her own good time; I wasn't about to pressure her into saying what was on her mind. Especially when I hadn't told her everything about Jacob, either… like the parts where I was started to fall for him, regardless of his macho-caveman attitude and his comments from earlier in the day. I didn't want to see her pitying looks or listen to her lecture on how I shouldn't fall for every guy I slept with. "So," I said instead. "What are you going to do? What's the plan?"

"The plan? It's pretty simple, really. First we're going to get smashed." Cara paused, taking a sip of her beer after we clinked bottles. "Then I'm going to open my own practice, and you're going to join me. Simple," she said with a nod as if it were a done deal. I had to admit it was a pretty tempting offer.

"Seriously? Easy as that?" I asked. Cara nodded again and fiddled with the label on her beer bottle. When we were going into our final year of grad school, she and I had thrown around the notion of opening a practice together, but without any experience under our belts, we both felt it was too ambitious.

"Yeah, I think we would be good partners, you know? Think about it, Lucia. We can be our own bosses, choose our clients—concentrate on different areas of expertise if we wanted to. But saying that, I've already done the research. There are hardly any private practices for children around here, and you already excel with the sports clientele."

"No I don't," I muttered, thinking of all my failures lately. It was something I liked to do, though, being around the stadium so much of my life. I could broaden it to baseball players, golfers, or even go the other way, target high-profile business people, stockbrokers, politicians… the possibilities were endless. No more coaches with God complexes breathing down my neck, no more smart-ass football players who were forced to come see me, who all thought it was a big joke and a waste of time. Instead, the client would come voluntarily and want the help I could provide.

"Just think about it, okay?" Cara was saying, a smile playing on her lips as if she knew I was already doing just that.

"I'll definitely think about it," I replied. I lifted up my drink and took a healthy swig. This could be the opportunity I was looking for.

Chapter Fifteen
JACOB

I was in a foul mood and not really wanting to talk with anyone. I'd received three more calls from *him*. The first two I'd left to go to voicemail, but the last one caught me off guard. I was hurrying to the locker room, running late, thinking perhaps it was Coach, and without checking the I.D. I picked up.

"It's about goddamn time you answered." The voice ran through me like ice. "Don't even think about hanging up. We have a lot to discuss. Like where's my fucking money, you piece of shit?" Old habits die hard, and the little boy in me couldn't make the move to end the call.

"What do you want?" I asked, my brain unable to function.

"Are you deaf as well as stupid? I want my money. I want what I'm owed! And if you don't pay up, I'm coming to get it."

The sounds of other players, loud with chatter, bounced noisily around the locker room, finally bringing me out of my dazed state. I closed my eyes and willed myself to say the words. "You're not getting a damn cent from me," I said and ended the call.

I sat heavily on the wooden bench beside my locker and tried to close up the anger and frustration that had leaked out in the last few minutes. But that wasn't all that was on my mind. I had more pressing things to worry about. It had been nearly four weeks since I had spoken with Lucia, and dammit, my dreams were filled with her. There were many times I had picked up the phone to call her or text her, even, but I chickened out each time, not really sure what to say. All I knew was that I was damn miserable without seeing her at least one time in last few weeks. I had screwed up, and I didn't know how to fix it in the slightest. At least, though, thinking of her was distracting me from the other relentless phone calls and stupid notes I kept receiving from my admirer.

Another note had appeared on my windshield that morning, the envelope containing one naked photograph of a woman with huge knockers bending seductively for the camera. Her number was on the back. She was hot but reeked of desperation.

"Yo, Jacob, what's kicking?"

I looked up to find Terrence next to me, his smiling face irritating me even more. Hell, he was part of the reason I was in such a mess in the first place. Him and that damn playbook of his. The only good thing was that he had paid me his grand already, or I would have planted a fist in his face. "What?"

"Whoa," Terrence replied, holding up his hands in surrender. "What's wrong with you?"

"Nothing," I grumbled as we made it to our lockers, thinking that I needed something more than a beer to calm my nerves. But I shook off the temptation to ask him to borrow the playbook for a moment. An easy lay would take the edge off, yet I had a feeling that still wouldn't do the trick. No, I needed to focus on the game and the following practice, which was going to get me the top spot. "Think Coach will run our asses off today?"

Terrence shrugged as he threw his bag into his locker, clearly not worried about it. After all, that was what he was paid to do. "You can't fool me,

Jake. You've been moody as hell for weeks. Is this about the doctor? Aren't you over her yet?"

I sighed, really not wanting to talk about it at all. Lucia was my business, not the team's. But surely I had to tell someone before I exploded?

"You should let her roll off of your shoulders, man, go stick your dick in someone else. Take your mind of her," he continued before I could answer, pulling his shirt over his head and saving me from embarrassing myself. "If you don't get your head in the game, you could lose your spot. Either that or man up. Go get what you want and damn the consequences. It's your life; you only get one."

I leaned forward, elbows on my thighs and rubbed my hands over my face, feeling drained. Maybe the idiot—who I'd fondly started to consider a friend—next to me was right. I could lose my job if I didn't get my head stuck on right. Forgetting her was the right thing to do. Move on... there was more pussy around the corner, and plenty more fishes that didn't come with all the baggage that she had. After all, it was clear that Lucia didn't care about what had happened between us, either. For the most part she'd been staying clear of me.

Grabbing my stuff, I walked out to the practice field by myself, needing the space to refocus.

Pre-season was just around the corner, and if I wanted that starting position, I was going to have to work my ass off for it. I had something to prove, and I shouldn't let some woman—a one-night stand, even—get in the way of me rising to the top.

* * *

Practice was brutal, the sun overly hot. If I hadn't known better I would've sworn it was like two hundred degrees outside instead of the ninety-degree weather that it actually was—even the grass was beginning to scorch. Wiping my face with my shirt, I walked down the hall, feeling the burn in my shoulder from the throwing reps I had done. Ahead of me Lucia walked down the passageway toward me, her attention buried in the papers in her hands. She looked gorgeous, and I felt my heart begin to race as she drew near. What was I going to say? I wanted to say something good, anything to get her attention.

She looked up and I froze, seeing the recognition in her eyes. A myriad of emotions crossed her face, and I swallowed hard, trying to form the words on my tongue. *Say something, dammit!*

Instead, I watched as she averted her gaze and hurried past me before I could say anything at all. For a moment I stood there in the hall, the smell of her sweet, addictive perfume still lingering in the air.

Shit. I had blown that one. How the hell was I going to fix this? Did I want to fix it?

My legs did the talking; I ran down the hall and grabbed her arm just before she reached her door. "Lucia, dammit, slow down. Jeez, you can walk fast when you want to."

She turned, and I could see tears in her eyes, socking me in the gut unexpectedly. "Just leave me alone," she said tightly, wrenching her arm out of my grasp and walking into her office, shutting the door behind her. I heard her engage the lock and I stood there, trying ever so desperately to understand those tears. *Fuck.* The last thing I wanted to do was hurt her.

But it was done… and she clearly didn't want to see me again, and I wasn't about to break down her door and get myself fired in the process. Fine. Whatever it was, it was over. I'd tried, *hadn't I?*

I retreated and collapsed on the bench in front of my locker. I sat there for a moment, my head swimming from the practice and from the close encounter with Lucia. Maybe I *should* pick another girl out of the book to get her off of my mind. I reached into Terrence's locker—it was still safely stashed near the back—and I pulled it down, holding it in my hands. This book had gotten me into some pretty deep shit, and I didn't know if I wanted to have that happen again.

And a small part of me, mainly my idiotic lower region, protested giving up Lucia so quickly. She was a wonderful woman who was misunderstood, and I hated the fact that I had to be so nonchalant about our fleeting relationship now that I knew she was the owner's daughter. I half thought about striding down to her office again, breaking the door down this time—regardless of the consequences—and hashing out this issue between us, preferably against her desk with her long legs up in the air, until we were both spent. Now that would be a therapy session I could get behind.

Sliding my shirt over my head, I grabbed a towel and headed to the shower. A cold shower was going to be miserable but much needed, given my state.

Chapter Sixteen
LUCIA

I leaned against the door trying to figure out where I had gone wrong in my life to deserve such a mess. My heart was in turmoil and my brain, well, that was definitely not functioning properly. After running into Jacob in the hall, I had to retreat to my office in an effort to calm my beating heart, hating the fact that he had that kind of effect on me even though we hadn't seen each other nor conversed in a number of weeks. I'd been good so far at avoiding him but I hadn't realized how miserable I had been about not seeing him until now, missing him way more than I should.

Pushing away from the door, I walked over to my chair and sat down, looking sadly at my calendar. On it were a number of red marks, signifying all of the players who had not shown up for their appointments. I didn't know if the word had gotten out that Greg had put down stipulations on which players had to see me or not, but the only people I had seen lately were some of the other support staff, including the office personnel who worked with me every day. Not a single player.

With a groan I laid my head on the desk and fought the urge to scream. This was not how my job was supposed to go! I wanted to help athletes, not be shunned by them! I wanted them to trust me, not laugh at me. Why had I thought that I could make a difference in this predominantly man-driven world? How did I ever think they were going to take me seriously? Without their coach believing in me or what I could provide for them, it was pointless, and as soon as my father found out about this boycott of sorts, it was going to be over. So why keep going? Cara's offer kept flitting around in my mind, tempting me, calling to me.

Picking my head up off the desk, I leaned back in my chair and spun it around to look out the window, tapping my fingers against the arms of the chair. Perhaps it was time to call it quits, to move on, and maybe now was the perfect time to take Cara up on her offer. It wasn't like anyone was going to miss me here anyway. Jacob's stone-cold expression and inability to say anything worthwhile told me all I needed to know. I had been stupid to let my guard down, to think I could find a good guy in a player. He was no different than the rest of them. I had put my faith in a man who couldn't give me what I needed—but to be fair it was my own fault. I'd gotten my hopes up too soon, too fast, and all because of one night, some mind-blowing sex, and a few knee-knocking words whispered into my ear.

* * *

"The team looks good, don't they?"

I nodded as I watched the offense on the field from the sidelines. One of the perks of being the owner's daughter was that I had a permanent field pass for any home game (not to mention access to the owner's private box, of course), and another pass for all the away games if I chose to travel with the team to cheer them on. And on many occasions I had flown with my father to the away games, my love of the sport just as intense as his. But tonight was just a pre-season home game, and my father and I had walked down to the field as the fourth quarter drew closer to the end, our guys up by a touchdown.

Together we stood near the end zone, my father watching his investments closely as they trotted on and off the field, looking for any signs of injuries or any setbacks that might make the season a rough one. So far, everyone looked great; most of the starters were on the bench with the exception of the quarterback. I had waited with bated breath to see Jacob trot out on the field and show off his skill set, but Greg had only put him in to cover one play when Danny Miller, the star, needed a breather.

"I think you have a good one, Dad, two actually," I finally said as we watched Danny take a knee for the final play. The win was ours.

My dad grinned and walked over to Greg to congratulate him on the win as I looked over to try and find Jacob amongst the celebrating players. He was nowhere in sight, and I frowned, wondering where he had gotten off to so quickly. We needed to talk so badly; I was tired of this helpless feeling, but perhaps this wasn't the right time. Yet, if not now, when?

We were both adults, and we really should be able to be civil to one another, perhaps grown-up enough to sit down at a table (one with dinner, I thought hopefully) and discuss whatever it was that was between us. It wasn't a relationship, I knew that—I wasn't that bloody naive—but it was far more than just a one-night stand as well. I wasn't blind to the fact that I craved Jacob, and maybe he was feeling the same way. I shook my head. Was I really contemplating a casual relationship with a player? Was I that desperate? No, that wasn't it. I'd just had a taste of something, and I wanted more… a lot more. And I was beginning to realize I was willing to do anything for it. For him.

God, I was a goner.

Greg and my father strolled back over towards me and I gave the coach the best smile I could muster, given the circumstances of our previous meeting. "Good game, Greg."

"Thank you, Lucia," he replied, very aware that he was standing next to the man who held his job in his hands. I felt like if my dad hadn't been there, he would have persisted with his animosity. It was funny to see him pretend to like me, when I knew he couldn't care less. He nodded to both of us, made his excuses and left in the direction of the locker room, following a long line of players hurrying off the field, leaving my father and me standing on the sideline.

"How about I take my favorite daughter out for a meal?" my father asked, putting his hands in his pockets. He was wearing what I called his casual clothes, a pair of jeans and a golf shirt that had the team's emblem on the left side, his reading glasses hanging around his neck. We had made him get them a few years ago, Merry complaining that he was squinting too much. He had balked at the idea, but in the end, Merry always won out.

"I'm your only daughter," I said with a smile. "Thanks for the offer, but I'm really tired, Dad. Rain check?" I finally said, not really wanting to have any company right then. I just wanted to go home, get into my pajamas, and bury my sorrows in my favorite ice cream.

"Of course, honey," he replied, returning my smile, though the frown line crossing his forehead never disappeared. "You go on home and rest."

I gave him a quick hug and decided to do just that. Remembering I had left a file in my office that I wanted to take home to dictate, I took a quick detour through the facility. The hallway was dark as I walked to my office; the place was quiet now that the game was over. But there was still a hum of activity coming from the locker room and training rooms that echoed down the corridors. Coaches and players would be in there, cooling down, going over the game and tending to any injuries before everyone could go home for the night. The actual season was a vicious cycle of extremely busy weekends as they prepped for the games, the culmination of the hard work by everyone seen on Sundays and of course Monday nights, when thousands of people in the stadium and millions worldwide enjoyed a good game of football.

"Doc."

I closed my eyes briefly as I let his voice register in my head. That low voice which had sent vibrations through my entire body not so long ago. My heart beat loudly in my ears. No, not now! I couldn't do this right now, I wasn't prepared.

"Lucia?"

Against my better judgment I turned around and faced Jacob, who was mere feet away, still dressed in his uniform, a serious look on his face. "Are you following me?" I asked, my voice hollow. He shook his head, gripping his helmet in his hands. "I'm not, I swear it."

I crossed my arms over my chest and glared at him. "Then why are you here?"

He ran a hand through his hair roughly. "Hell, I don't know, Doc. I really don't know. I can't keep away from you anymore. You're like a fucking magnet…" he trailed off and took a step forward, as if proving his statement.

I swallowed hard as I heard the indecision in his voice, as if he was torn between the team and being with me. I didn't want that. I didn't need that, and I didn't need him. Did I? I wished that I could stop lying to myself.

"One night wasn't enough, Lucia. I need to have you again," he continued, his voice getting louder with each word. What if someone overheard us? What if we were caught together like this, unable to explain anything at all?

"I can't do this," I finally said, panic rising in my throat. Against everything I had ever said or done, I was actually starting to believe I needed him… my body surely did. I was buzzing with electricity with him being so close. I could reach out and touch him… feel him under my fingers again. And oh, how I wanted to. He was saying all the right things, acting like a normal human being, though perhaps he would say anything to have what he wanted. He had charm by the bucket load, and surely I would end up being just another notch on his bedpost again?

I was so fucking torn, I felt like I was being ripped in two. As I stared into his pleading eyes— eyes that told me he would have me right here in the corridor if I let him—I nearly gave in. But it was the taboo nature of our relationship that was messing everything up; my career and reputation depended on me not going against the rules. It was too important. I'd worked far too hard to let it all go to waste for a *man*. I couldn't risk it. I couldn't fail.

"Let's go talk, or…" he said, taking another step forward. Sweat and spice wrapped around me like a cloud. He smelled so good.

"I'm sorry," I said, almost as a whisper.

"No wait, Luce," he started as I turned around and started to jog away in the direction of the entrance, hoping he wouldn't follow because I wasn't sure if I could say no and turn him away again. I wasn't strong enough for that. Screw the file. I couldn't deal with Jacob Maddox tonight.

Chapter Seventeen
JACOB

I leaned against the bar, a half bottle of beer in my hand as I watched the crowd partying below. Some of the players intermingled with the hot chicks who were looking for that one easy ride for the night. After the big win the guys wanted to go clubbing, so we had ended up in a VIP section in the club Destination, high above the dance floor. A bevy of gorgeous young women were already waiting for our arrival at the top of the stairs.

I'd accepted a few congratulations and more than one hand on my ass, but it was difficult to get into the party mood. Gone was the need to fuck any warm body; instead I kept out of the limelight and brooded by myself. It was funny to see the way both sexes used each other for their own gains, and in the end it was rare that anything serious came of it. I was a bit surprised at how I viewed the entire mess tonight, how petty the act of a hookup seemed now that I had experienced a taste of something more.

"Dude, are you going to nurse that beer all night?" Terrence asked, his voice loud over the pumping music as he sipped on his drink. He lounged on the nearby chair with a woman on his lap—she looked like she was there for the duration. "You've only been holding it for the last hour."

"What are you, the drink police?" I shot back, in no mood for joking. Let him have his booze and women, I was content to sit here and think. But I was regretting having come. I should have gone straight home after cleaning up, but the guys had talked me into celebrating the win I had very little part in, so I'd caved, thinking it would do me some good to spend some time with the boys and that perhaps a night out would clear my head. But hell, it had only made it worse.

"Chill, dude," Terrence replied, his eyes narrowing. "What's eating you? You pissed the coach didn't put you in more?"

I shrugged. To be truthful, I was a little pissed about that, thinking that if I'd only gotten a minute or two more in the game I could've shown him what I was made of. On the ride over, the sports radio presenters had a field day with me, calling me an expensive benchwarmer and a one-hit wonder. That just added fuel to the fire, and now not only did I want to kick some ass, I wanted to show them that I was better than they perceived me to be. I could be that starter again, I just needed the chance and more than a few plays to get going.

"You know I heard that the doc is going to be gone by the end of the week," Terrence said as we stood watching the party below us. "The boycott is in full force."

"What?" I replied, surprised. "Why?"

"He doesn't want her around," he said with a shrug. "Says she interferes too much, scrambling our brains and shit. I will be glad not to have to go sit through an hour of touchy-feely anymore."

"She's just trying to help," I fired back, knowing deep down that I had caused this the moment. I had said something about her messing with my head in an attempt not to face her. Hell, she was going to really hate me now. No wonder she didn't want to talk to me. I was about to cost her her job over some stupid words I'd said without thinking it all through. Dammit, I didn't mean to screw her job up, as well.

"You haven't given her a chance to help you."

Terrence looked at me funny, a grin spreading over his lips. "You're sticking up for her. Dude, what did she do in that bed? Spin you like a helicopter?"

"Shut the hell up," I growled. Friend or no friend, I was not going to let him talk about Lucia that way. She didn't deserve it. Her heart was in the right place, and if they would give her even a half a chance to do her job, then everyone else would see it, as well. My eyes widened; it was as if a light had flickered into life in my head. I was a damn fool. I had thought the exact same thing, had practically bribed her into a date in order to win the bet, but had I lived up to my end of the bargain? Had I been open-minded enough to go through with a session? Had I fuck... no, instead I did what I always did: I thought about number one and to hell with everyone else. I hadn't thought what would happen. Typical fucking jock, I thought, despising myself.

"Fine, hey, I can't afford to get into a fight tonight, and I suppose in a way those sessions weren't all that bad... they got me pumped up for practice—even more so than normal when I think on it," Terrence said, holding up his drink as the girl drifted her hands over his broad shoulders in silent invitation.

"But anyway, come on man, how about you just lay off of it for a while? This chick is really screwing with both of your heads. Go get yourself another girl and get her out of your system. That's the best thing to do, right? Unless…"

"Unless, what?"

He glanced at me, his mouth partially open as if he were about to say something more. "Nah, never mind."

I broke the stare and set the beer on the counter. "I don't want another girl. This one is trouble enough," I said, mostly to myself, but Terrence heard and gave a little shrug. I reached into my pocket and pulled out my keys, feeling suddenly tired. "I'm out, dude. Have a good one."

"All right, man, see you tomorrow," Terrence said as I walked past him, throwing him a quick wave before heading for the stairs down. Outside the club, the night was balmy and blissfully quiet. My ears felt like they'd been about to burst from the noise—perhaps out here I could actually think. I wandered over to where my car was parked and noticed something trapped under the arm of one of the wipers. What looked to be a small rectangular sheet flapped in the breeze, the edges catching the wind and furling upwards.

Not this again.

I snatched at what I now realized was an envelope, took one glance at it before I shuddered—the back was sealed, and along the edge were two kisses, ruby red lip-prints stamped upon the paper. I couldn't deal with this, either, I thought. I quickly crumpled the envelope, and the letter and picture that was no doubt inside, with my fist and let it fall to the ground. I stood for a second with my eyes closed and pushed the envelope and its sender far from my mind.

With that dealt with and my head reasonably clear, I climbed in, closing the door hard behind me. I gripped the wheel with my hands, telling myself that I needed to point the car in the direction of home before I did something really stupid. The thought of Lucia still lingered. It was like I'd been bitten, and no amount of scratching was going to make the itch subside. I tried to tell myself there was no way in hell I was going to walk up to her father's house, my boss' home, just to see her. That would be the worst move ever. Do not pass go, do not collect $200; go directly to jail and kiss my NFL career goodbye. No, I had to wait until she came to me. I didn't have any other options.

With a sigh I turned over the engine, peeled out of the parking lot, and made the sensible decision to go home. My realtor had managed to get us through the closing in super quick time, and now with the help of an interior decorator, the place was fully furnished. Except it didn't really feel *full*. Without Lucia there, the place was like an echoey cavern. Yes, I could have all the toys and gadgets I wanted, enough to fill the whole damn house if I wanted to, but something was missing. I couldn't even use the damn pool! I hated this, but I hated being separated from Lucia even more. Fuck's sake, how could I let myself get so hung up on one woman after only knowing her for such a short time? It was like a prank was being pulled on me, and for a second I considered that this was probably how all my past groupies and conquests felt… How was I going to fix this? Did I even have what it took to make it right? I'd been wrong and the coach was wrong, and there had to be some way to have my cake and eat it, too.

I pulled up in the drive and shut the engine off before climbing the stairs to the empty, quiet house. Lucia had been right—it was far too big for just one person. The evening was close, and if there were any night to have a dip in the pool and forget about her, it would be tonight, but I couldn't find enough energy to even want to strip off my clothes. Opening the door, I threw my keys into the new bowl on the foyer table— neither of which I had picked out—and walked

183

into the kitchen. I pulled a beer out of the fridge before noticing that the pool lights were on. I walked out onto the patio to investigate, though knowing myself I probably just forgot to turn them off.

The glow from the pool wasn't enough to obscure the brightness of the stars tonight, and the waterway looked as if it were lit up with twinkling strands. My eyes sought the gentle ripple of the pool's surface. Water normally soothed me, but tonight I still felt restless, especially after finding the note on my car. Instead of dwelling on it, my mind drifted to Lucia again. What was she doing right now? Sleeping, no doubt, or at least I hoped so. Shame it was the wrong bed.

Suddenly I caught movement out of the corner of my eye., then heard a splash. A figure was hiding in the shadows at the far end of the pool, near the jacuzzi.

I swallowed, ready to bolt, but something made me stay. If it was *him* or a burglar, would they really be using the pool? And the outline of the person, now coming towards me, was relatively small. The hourglass shape of woman. *Could it be?*

I waited, almost not breathing as the figure ducked down beneath the surface and slowly drifted forward, swimming through the water.

She made it to the far edge and emerged in one smooth motion, head, then bare shoulders coming up next.

I couldn't believe my eyes.

Her smile was wide; pleased at my reaction… though she wouldn't be soon enough. But still my eyes were glued to her dripping wet naked body as she rose out of the water, slowly taking one step at a time, so I could take my time to appreciate the view. But the view was soured…

"What the fuck are you doing here?"

"Oh, honey. Don't you like your surprise?" she said, her hands outstretched, showcasing every last inch of her frame. Her hands came back to her sides, trailing up her torso, then up to her huge breasts, squeezing them together. "This is all for you, Jakey."

I had to force myself to look away—I was still a hot-blooded man after all. But here was a forbidden fruit standing before me, ripe, and ready for plucking, fucking, and everything in between.

Except the woman who was eager and very willing wasn't Lucia.

She was my very own stalker.

* * *

"Isabella," I started.

"See, you do care, you remembered my name," she said, almost purring the words. "You can call me Izzy, though, if you prefer. Actually you can call me anything you want while you're fucking me."

"It's hard to forget when you've sent me countless cards, texts, and emails all signed with your name, oh and yes, not forgetting the naked pics. Mind, the team did love those."

She frowned. The night obviously wasn't going as she'd planned. "I don't understand, Jakey. Didn't you like them, too? They were for *you*. You liked me well enough when we were in the limo… And you did promise me a rain check."

Izzy sashayed forwards, tiny droplets parting from her tight and well-maintained body before she came to a stop in front of me.

Before I could stop her she cupped my hard cock—the traitor—and started rubbing. "See, you want me. I know you do. Let's go play…"

Where I found the willpower to stop her I didn't know. But Lucia's face kept darting into view in my mind's eye.

"No. Stop. Enough's enough. You do realize I could get you fired over this?"

"You wouldn't!" she gasped.

"Try me."

Her face was full of fury now; it was clear she wasn't going to get what she wanted.

"Come on, you have to leave. Where are your clothes?"

A devilish smile appeared on her lips. "I don't know," she said unconvincingly.

"Seriously? Well, in that case you'll just have to get home naked."

I grabbed her by the elbow and started to lead her to the house. Thankfully she followed willingly without struggling. But she didn't stop telling me all the things I could do to her, if only I would let her stay. She was giving everything up on a platter, but for some reason it no longer appealed. We reached the front door, but I stopped before I opened it. No matter what I'd said, I couldn't throw her out like she was. I wasn't that much of a prick.

I started to pull my shirt off over my head and her eyes widened with glee. "No," I said, quickly putting a stop to the dirty thoughts that were no doubt whizzing through her peroxide-addled mind. "Put this on."

She pouted but did what I said. "You're no fun anymore." The shirt was huge, swamping her frame and coming down to just above her knees, but at least she was covered now and less tempting.

"Did you drive or come in a taxi?"

"Taxi," she muttered.

"Fine, I'll order you an Uber."

A few moments later I was letting in the car and escorting her down the steps. I wanted to make sure she was going to get in and not hide and try get back into the house. I wouldn't put it past her to wait till I was asleep and slip into bed next to me.

Preoccupied with Izzy, I failed to notice the second car pull up the drive until it was too late. I opened the back door of the Uber for her, but before she got in, Izzy wrapped her arms around my neck in a strong vise-like grip and then proceeded to kiss me. I managed to peel her off and placed her into the car without much difficulty after she'd gotten a taste of me. She grinned, waving at me from inside the dark interior of the luxury car. She mouthed the words "See you later, call me!"

I shook my head and wiped my mouth with the back of my hand. She was unbelievable… didn't give up.

It was then I looked up and properly registered the other car.

Lucia's partially lit face glared at me from inside her vehicle.

"No," I shouted. "It's not what you think, I promise!" But I had to know exactly what it looked like; I was half-dressed, and I'd just put a half-naked girl, who was wearing my freakin' shirt, into a cab after she'd slobbered all over me.

To my surprise, Lucia climbed out and stood with her arms across her chest. At least she hadn't driven away, I thought.

"Okay, listen to me. She's crazy. She's been following me everywhere, sending me notes, texts, harassing me, basically—"

"Like a stalker?" Lucia asked, her tone even and deadly.

"Yes! Exactly like that. I came home and she was in my house! In the pool, naked! I thought it was you! You have to believe me."

She quirked her eyebrow at that, and I at once scolded myself. "You thought that piece of plastic was me?"

"I didn't mean… Fuck. It was dark, okay? And what was I to do? She wouldn't tell me where she'd hidden her clothes, so I had to give her mine. I promise I'm not making this up."

"I believe you."

"She was trying everything to get me to—wait, you believe me? I don't understand." I was thoroughly confused. Was this a trick?

The corners of her lips tugged slightly upwards as she gave a shrug. "It happens more than you think. That was Isabella, right?"

I nodded, dumbfounded.

"Yeah, you probably want to stay away from that one. She has a bit of a reputation for getting, shall we say, *attached* to the new players."

"Okay, good to know. So why are you here?"

"I don't really know. I was driving around, and I kinda ended up here. Silly, huh?"

"No, I don't think it's silly. Do you want to come inside?"

"I shouldn't," she said far too quickly, as if I'd startled her out of a daze. "I shouldn't even be here. I don't know what I was thinking." She opened her car door as if to get back in and leave.

Grasping at straws, not wanting her to go, I said the first that popped out. "Running back to Daddy? God forbid you do anything that you want to do."

She glowered at me. *What the fuck, dude?*

Insulting her wasn't going to win you any brownie points.

"Low blow, Jacob." And with that she was back in her car, driving away so fast her tires lost traction and threw up a shower of gravel.

Chapter Eighteen
LUCIA

"Lucia! You have a delivery!"

I climbed off of the couch and hurried to the front door, where Merry was holding a beautiful vase of roses, the darkest red I had ever seen. Normally I would have been at the guest house, but this morning I couldn't help but want to be around someone and had come up to the main house for Sunday breakfast with Merry and my father. He was upstairs preparing to make his customary run to the stadium for his end-of-the-week meeting, while Merry and I planned to catch up on our shows on the DVR while we pampered ourselves with pedicures for a bit. Once Dad returned, then he would take us for a nice, leisurely lunch, as he did most Sundays.

"Oh, they are beautiful," I breathed as she handed over the vase. There had to be two dozen of them, if not more, and amongst the lush green foliage was an envelope attached to a stem with my name scrawled across it in big looping swirls. It had been a long time since I had received flowers on anything but a special occasion, and curiosity was killing me to know who had sent them… but I wouldn't let myself get my hopes up. That was the road to disaster. He was still a jerk, a Neanderthal without a filter. *But what if…?*

"Who are they from?" Merry asked as we walked back into the kitchen. I set the crystal vase gently on the countertop and removed the envelope. I slid a fingernail under it, holding my breath as I was about to pull out the card. "A secret admirer, perhaps? Or was it your hot date from last month? Which reminds me, you never told me how it went. Have you seen him again? Must've been some night to make you nearly miss your father's campaign speech."

"It went, er, fine," I replied, not wanting to elaborate and praying that my cheeks wouldn't give me away. What was I going to tell her anyway? That I had slept with a player and gotten my heart broken all in one fell swoop?

Pulling out the card, I read the inscription:

I'm so sorry, was all it said, signed with the initials J.M.

Jacob had sent me flowers; beautiful, delicate flowers. It had to be him; there was no one else in my life with those initials. He was apologizing, but could I trust the words on the card? I'd walked away from him twice now, tearing myself away more like it, and I thought that would be the end of it, that he'd want nothing to do with me after that. And yet he sent me these? Talk about mixed signals. *No, Lucia, stop it. Stop reading into things. He's just saying sorry for being a douchebag. He knows you could easily snitch on him to your father. He's just making sure you don't. He isn't declaring his love for you.*

I was probably right, it was nothing. He was probably only apologizing for his uncalled-for comment back at his house and for backing out of our long-forgotten deal.

"J.M.?" Merry asked as she read the card over my shoulder. "Who's that?"

"Oh, no one you know…"

"J.M? I recognize those initials! Lucia Cortes, I better be one hundred percent wrong." I turned around to find my father staring me down, several deep creases on his sun-kissed face. "That better not be Jacob Maddox," he continued, his words and the mere mention of Jacob's name making me freeze in my place.

"Who? What? No... No, of course not," I sputtered, feeling nauseated. "That's ridiculous, Daddy. Why would Jacob Maddox be sending me flowers?" Merry's eyebrow rose up into those perfected arches of hers, and I silently willed her to be quiet, knowing that she could see straight through my lies. She had a gift for it.

"There have been rumblings about you two," my father said as he snatched the card out of my hands and read it again. Never had I been so excited to have a florist fill out a card in all my life. No identifying signature, no phone number attached so that it could be traced back.

"You must be thinking of someone else," I said desperately. Rumblings? What the hell?! What had he heard?

"Well, it's highly suspicious. 'I'm so sorry'? What did this person do to you?"

"I don't know," I said, biting my lip hard to keep from breaking down and confessing to everything. But still, Jacob had sent me flowers. That had to mean something. And though one half of me was on the verge of tears from being found out, it was hard to keep the happy voice on the other side from bursting into song and dancing around the kitchen.

"Probably just a client…missed their appointment or something."

He narrowed his eyes as he handed the card back to me, distrust in his gaze but a slight smile on his face. "Well, then you must be having a good effect on them for them to send you apology flowers. I'm proud of you. I knew you'd make a success out of it. Of course I had my doubts at the start, but you're really doing it."

I gave him a smile, feeling all kinds of horrible inside as he walked away. If only he knew the real truth. I was doing a shitty job, but at least no one had complained to him… yet.

Picking up the vase to take them back to the guest house, I turned to say goodbye to Merry, but before I could open my mouth she was all over me.

"So, your father might've fallen for it, but I certainly did not. Spill, young lady."

I groaned. "Do we really have to do this now?" I hissed, hyper-aware that my father was still somewhere in the house and could be within earshot at any second.

"Yes. You're my only daughter and, well, I have to live vicariously through someone, now don't I?"

"It's a long story," I said and continued before she could interrupt me again, "one that I'm not ready to tell yet."

"But—"

"But! It's early stages, I don't want to jinx it. And these," I said as I hugged the vase, "these might very well be a sign that... Oh, I don't know, that he's not who I originally thought he was."

"I have no idea what any of that means, hon. The main thing is that he makes you happy. Does he?"

I couldn't hold back the blush any longer and shrugged, a nod following not far behind. It was the truth after all, the time spent with him alone had been wondrous, and even when we were fighting it was exquisite. But even I knew that I had to make sure I wasn't going into this with my head stuck in the sand—one night with him wasn't proof enough that we were meant to be. It would take a whole lot more than that.

Finally, Merry saw sense and let me go without pulling out any more interrogation tactics. I think she realized I still needed to work things out in my head before I could fully open up to her about it. I continued my walk contemplating what I should do next. What *would* be my next step? The ball was definitely in my court now, and if I didn't act soon, well, I was sure he would move on. After all, Isabella was waiting in the wings, waiting for any chance to scoop him up.

I could call him and tell him thank you, but I didn't want to talk to his voicemail again. We needed to discuss this face-to-face. But God help me if I did that. I would need a script of some sort to stop me from getting distracted. Last night when he'd been half-naked had been bad enough. My mouth went dry as I'd taken in his sculpted pecs and firm, tempting abs.

What if he didn't want to see me anymore? The question popped into my head out of nowhere, with dread following not far behind it. I was over-analyzing everything, I knew that, yet it was better to know all the angles before I went head first into something that could very well be another misunderstanding... Because what if these flowers were not "I'm sorry I fucked up" but more like "I'm sorry this isn't going to work out"?

The whats and the whys were going to be the death of me.

Pushing open the door, I set the flowers on the white oak coffee table and stared at them a long while, my thumb and forefinger brushing the card over and over again. I pulled out my phone and dialed Cara's number. She picked up on the first ring. "Hello?"

"He sent me flowers," I started, taking in a breath.

"He, who? Oh, your lover quarterback," she answered. "What kind are they?"

"Roses, lots of them," I said slowly. "Why do you ask?"

"The type of flowers a man sends a woman means a lot," Cara replied, playful irritation in her voice. "Come on, Lucia, get with the program. So roses, well, let's see here. What color?"

"Red, an intense crimson," I said, still staring at them, lost in their beauty.

"Oh, really? Passion, love... sex."

"Be serious!" I laughed.

"I am. It means he's a very deep romantic type and that he keeps his emotions hidden until either he wants something or he really likes someone. Probably both in this case, I guess. Plus, red symbolizes all that good stuff I mentioned before. It's a clear message really, Luce. He's sending you a jolt of energy and hoping it flows back to him. In other words, he wants to fuck your brains out."

"Are you Googling that?" I asked with a laugh. "Or have you turned into some type of new-age botanist?"

"Shut up," she said, "and listen to me. I can help you through this."

"Okay. You need to tell me what my next step should be. I don't trust myself anymore," I snapped, wanting quick answers. "Should I call him?"

"Hell no. You should go and see him," she replied. "He's still interested. Stop thinking, Luce. Go show him what he's missing out on and call me when you get done. I want to hear all the juicy details."

I rolled my eyes. "You're such a bad influence!" I replied then said goodbye, setting the phone down on the table before looking at my watch. It was a little after ten in the morning. It was a little early for a visit but I couldn't wait, and I was under strict orders from my therapist, I thought with a wry smile. I could go extend the olive branch and offer to take him out for breakfast or brunch. With that snap decision made—or made for me—I went to change. I pulled out some jeans and a casual but still cute tank top. I wasn't going to know how it ended if I didn't at least try.

* * *

Jacob's home was just as I remembered it; last night it had been shrouded in darkness, but this morning it was absolutely stunning. The gate was wide open again and bravely I drove right in. Even the short distance up the driveway was breathtaking. No wonder he had put in an offer straight away.

As the front door came into view, I frowned; I saw two men in the driveway, their stances full of tension and anger. At least it wasn't another half-naked chick, I thought. One of them I quickly identified as Jacob, but the older man, for he had a touch of graying hair in his overgrown beard, I hadn't ever seen before. And yet there was something oddly familiar about him, too.

Muffled shouts made their way into the confines of my car, but I couldn't make out what they were saying. Either way, it wasn't good. Opening the door, I climbed out, worried. This definitely wasn't good. Was this another obsessed fan who was trying to accost Jacob? Twice in row didn't seem plausible, but didn't famous people get killed over things like that?

"You are a worthless son of a bitch! After everything I did for you, and you can't even find it in your heart to help me? What kind of family does that make you?"

I stopped in my tracks as Jacob's face turned red, from anger or embarrassment I didn't know. Both, I guessed. The other man was a few inches shorter than Jacob and had a slight pot belly that strained at his belt, but from my vantage point I could now make out some very similar features between the two men. Thick-set and wide shoulders, combined with a forthright nose and perfectly sized lips; they had to be related.

"Just go, you're not my family, *Dad*. Don't make me ask you again," Jacob said with a grimace. "You won't get anything from me. I told you to stay away. And don't make this out to be some sort of warm and fuzzy reunion because it never will be. I was done with you in Minnesota, years ago! And I'm done with you now."

Instead of turning around, his dad took a step forward, the short swing of his arm and the punch coming out of nowhere. I gasped as Jacob stumbled back; he was so fast on the field, but this was a pure sucker punch. There was no way he would've been able to dodge it. He brought a hand up to his lip that was now dotted with blood.

"That's right," his dad said, advancing another step toward him, "take it like you used to. Don't you ever forget I'm still your father. I can still beat the living shit out of you, doesn't matter how old you are." His dad was muttering now, the telltale ramble of a drunk. "Someone has to beat some sense into you, you entitled little shit. Think you can get rid of me that easily, huh? Think you're better than me?"

Jacob's fists balled up, and for a moment I thought he was going to strike back. Hell, I wanted to strike back for him. But instead he just stood there, his face mottled with rage and shame. I couldn't let his father take another swing at him. By the looks of it, if Jacob started swinging, he might not stop.

"Hey!" I shouted, getting both of their attention as I closed the gap between the pair and myself. "Leave him alone!"

"Who the hell is this?" his father said, his eyes narrowing, looking me up and down, like I was another fly to take a swat at. Jacob didn't answer, his eyes raking over me in both confusion and surprise. I came to stand between them, focusing my attention upon Jacob, my hands on my hips. The best way to deal with his father's kind was not to engage. "Did you forget about our breakfast plans?"

"I, no, what?" he said slowly, even more confused, and he looked over my shoulder.

"Breakfast. You and me, now."

"Hey, I'm talking here!"

I turned around and firmly addressed his father.

"You need to get out of here before the cops arrive."

"You little bitch. You're gonna regret this, Jacob. Your whore, too," his father said before stalking down the drive. "I'm not done with you yet, boy. You just wait and see." The man then disappeared around the corner, somehow managing to get past the gate that had closed behind me when I'd driven up, but at least he was gone for now. I waited a beat before I stole a glance at Jacob. His jaw was clenched, his lip split from his father's punch. He looked pissed.

"Are you okay?" I asked hesitantly, my heart aching and my hand reaching up to cup his face.

Chapter Nineteen
JACOB

She was here. Hell, Lucia was here and had just witnessed something I never wanted her or anyone to ever see. A part of my shame that I had desperately tried to hide. Her eyes were kind but full of questions as she looked at me, and I could feel the dull throb of my lip from where the man, Marshall Maddox, who'd helped conceive me, had struck. And not for the first time, either. I didn't consider him a father but a tyrant who had made my life a living hell.

"I'm fine," I said briskly, not wanting to show any weakness in front of her. It was bad enough that she'd seen me get hit and not fight back.

"Come on," she said, reaching for my hand, her soft voice music to my ears. "Let's get that cut cleaned up."

I wanted to tell her to leave, to go back to her cozy home with her perfect father, but a small piece of me, a rational part of me, couldn't force the harsh, jealous words past my lips. As much as I wanted to be alone, I also wanted to have her here. So, I wrapped my hand around hers and let her led us into the house, the cool interior a welcome relief from the muggy morning.

"You've added some things since I was here last," Lucia remarked as we walked past the living room and toward the kitchen, where I kept a first aid kit. I laughed, unable to help myself, and I felt some of the earlier tension start to ease off. "Just a few things. Now I can sit on a couch instead of the floor." Everything was finally moved into the space, and I was starting to get used to it being mine now.

"It looks good, Jacob," she smiled. Unable to help myself, I squeezed her hand before releasing it, pulling out the drawer that contained the kit. "Here, Doc," I said, pushing it across the counter. "Do your worst."

"Well," she said as she opened it and extracted what she needed, "It's a good thing you don't need stitches. I'm not that type of doctor, you know."

"You mean they didn't teach you that in school?" I teased as she drew close, dabbing the cut to clean it.

I focused on her eyes, the kindness in them nearly stealing my breath. I was glad she was here, damn glad. If she hadn't shown up when she had, I would've been in worse shit than I was right now.

"Trust me, you don't want me to do that," she said her face set to concentrating as she pulled the gauze away. "I can't sew a straight line to save my life, and I would hate to mess up your pretty face."

"You think my face is pretty, Doc?" I asked, enjoying the banter between us. Just talking to her again felt right. Reaching out, I grasped her wrist lightly; her pulse pounded under my thumb. "I think *you* are pretty fucking hot."

She blushed, and I grinned at her reaction. So at least I knew there was still something; all the time she'd ignored me or walked away, I knew it couldn't have been because there wasn't any attraction. There was shitloads of the stuff! Bringing her wrist up to my lips, I kissed it lightly, breathing in her scent. I wanted her. I could feel it all the way to my toes. It would take no time for me to get her undressed and bury myself in her warmth, to forget about what had just happened and everything else for a few moments at least. Her breath quickened as I released her wrist, and I thought she was thinking the same thing.

"Jacob? What happened out there?" she asked suddenly, killing my hard-on immediately. "Was that your father?"

"No," I said sharply, pulling away from her and walking to the fridge before she could finish dressing my cut. I stared inside the partially empty fridge, letting the cold air wash over me in an effort to regain my composure. "He's a glorified sperm donor. He's never been a father and never will be." I pulled out two bottles of water and turned back to her.

"I could tell you didn't get along very well, that was obvious," she responded as I turned back and set a bottle of water in front of her, drinking greedily from mine, mainly for something to do, something to keep my hands occupied. *Why on earth was I talking about this?*

"We don't," I replied after a moment. I had tried over the years to keep my personal life just that, personal. My father had approached me countless times over the years, butting in at the worst possible moments. He was like a virus I couldn't get rid of, but each time he reappeared I had to deal with him all over again. I thought I had made it clear to him that he wasn't going to get anything from me. The last time he had tried, God what a clusterfuck that had been. "I hate him. If the world was rid of him,

I wouldn't shed a tear. And how he found out my address, again, is beyond me."

"You're famous," she said, her lips pulling to the side in a slight grimace. "People will come out of the woodwork to be associated with you. You would be surprised what's available on the internet these days."

I had to agree with that. Literally my first month in professional football had thrust me into a spotlight that I probably wasn't ready for, and suddenly I had more relatives and friends than I cared to mention. It had taken the help of a damn good agent to keep me from handing out all of my well-earned fortune to them. "Speaking of which, you got my flowers? My note?"

She'd torn a piece of the label from her bottle of water and nodded.

"I am, you know? Sorry, I mean. For everything, for not talking to you or coming to see you all those weeks, but especially for the other night. You shouldn't have had to see that. But like you say, the crazies come out of the woodwork. And if I wasn't clear before she and I were definitely not doing you know…'cause we're most certainly not. Don't put your dick in crazy, like the saying goes," I said with an awkward laugh but Lucia kept silent.

"Who'd have thought I'd have my very own stalker? She's persistent and obsessed. I thought it was cute at first, following me everywhere around the facility, popping up at training like a love-struck puppy; it boosted my ego, I guess. But then it got creepy, you know? Like last night…"

Even though Lucia knew that Izzy was batshit crazy, I still wanted to make it clear to her that women like that who forced themselves into my life meant nothing to me. "And then shit, that thing I said to you about your dad. I didn't mean it. I just didn't want you to leave again."

She nodded and hope started to swell in my heart. Would she forgive me?

"You know, you should probably get a restraining order."

"I will," I said and took a step closer, edging around the kitchen island towards her.

"And I don't mean just one. I don't want anything to happen to you…"

That made me smile. "I promise, I will. It's about time I cut him out of my life for good, too. He was not and is not a very nice man," I finally said, figuring I needed to give her something so she would be satisfied with what had happened out there. "The best day of my life was when I could walk away from him and no longer be under his control."

Lucia didn't say anything for a moment, and I watched as she climbed off the stool she had been sitting on and walked over to me, closing the gap. She carefully placed her arms around my waist as she hugged me to her. "I'm sorry, Jacob," she replied. I let out a pent-up breath and threw my arms around her, burying my face into her hair. Though she was only giving me a hug, I felt like she understood my need not to talk about it. The pain of my childhood was not a topic that I readily liked to discuss.

"So, did you like them, my flowers?" I asked, struggling to steady the emotion in my voice. I had felt the need to do something after the awkwardness of our conversation last night at the stadium and then later when she'd turned up and witnessed me throwing Isabella half-dressed out of my house. The need to let her know that I wasn't going to stay completely away from her had intensified. I just had to figure out what the hell I was going to do about her being the owner's daughter.

"I did, and they were lovely. Maybe next time don't send them to the house, though," she said with a slight wince, pulling away from me.

"Oh shit, your father saw? Did he see the note? Fuck, I'm so stupid."

"No, I mean yes, he did, but no you're not stupid. It's okay, I covered for you."

"So he doesn't know?"

She shook her head. "I'm pretty sure you're not the only person out there with the initials J.M."

I let out a relieved breath. We were still in the clear. For now.

"It's why I came over, though. Want to get some brunch with me, so we can talk?"

"Brunch with you would be awesome," I grinned, already thinking about what we were going to do afterwards, if I had my way. I planned to spend the rest of the morning in bed with her. Then I would be a beast on the practice field that afternoon, knowing that everything was okay between us. God yes, I loved that plan.

I leaned in close, my hands on her arms, and stole a kiss. Not really caring about the pain or the swelling of my lip. I was gentle and it was over much too quick; I didn't want to ruin the moment by getting too hot and heavy. She wanted to talk, so that was what we were going to do. There would be time enough later for everything wicked I had running through my mind. But for now it was important that I did what she requested. I wanted to show her I could be more than what my cock could provide. I let her go and stepped back. The light in her eyes was bright, and she nibbled at her lip that I'd just kissed. "We should go," she said, a little breathless. I nodded; we had to go before I changed my mind.

"Will you grab my keys over on the counter? I'll be right back. Just want to change. We can take my car; I know just the place," I called to her as I quickly ran towards the stairs. In super quick time, like a superhero instantly shedding his clothes to don his costume, I changed out of my workout clothes into a pair of casual but respectable shorts and a polo shirt. With a glance in the bathroom mirror, I made sure the cut on my lip hadn't busted open before jogging back down to the first floor. It was knitting together slowly. I grinned regardless. This was what I needed, time spent with her. We'd sort out what we were going to do, how we were going to proceed with her father looming over us, and then we'd get to the good stuff.

As I rounded the corner, I saw that she was holding something small in her hands. "You ready?"

"Jacob," she said, holding up the book she was looking at. "What's this?"

Shit.

My world imploded.

No, not now.

I felt the grin slide from my face as I recognized the offending playbook in her hands, forgetting that I had stuffed it in my pocket after yesterday with the plan to burn it at the first opportunity. But I had a habit of dumping all of my pocket's contents into the new bowl by the door when I arrived home in the evenings, making sure that I kept everything together and that I could find my keys easily. *Fuck.* Damn that black book. Had she read the contents? I would have to talk fast to explain… The entire thing was damn ridiculous, and I'd wanted to get rid of all the things that others had written about her.

"I, um nothing," I stammered, the cogs of my mind sticky with molasses. They wouldn't work, how the fuck was I going to explain this? I walked towards her, my hands up in submission, hoping she wouldn't bolt. She bit her lip and flipped the open book around, hurt registered all over her face as she jabbed at the entry with her name on it. *Dammit!*

"My name is in here, with a big X over it. Care to comment on that one?"

"Let me explain, Lucia… this is just like Izzy, a simple misunderstanding. You let me explain that one, let's sit down and talk. I'll tell you everything," I pleaded, reaching for the book. She was much more than what that damn book said. I didn't want her for any bet anymore, I wanted her because she was Lucia, and she kept me on my toes. She made me feel worthy for a change. She pulled it out of my grasp and tucked it in her pocket out of reach.

"All this time I wondered why you had taken such an interest in me, and now I know."

"Please, no, it's not like that. If you'd just let me explain," I pleaded, reaching for her now. The hurt in her eyes was tearing my heart in two. "You are fucking amazing. The guys who wrote those comments didn't even know the real you."

"So where are your comments?" she asked, her voice barely above a whisper, tears glimmering in her eyes. It made me feel like pond scum, no, even worse than that. I never wanted to hurt her. "What were you going to write? 'An easy lay if you are nice to her'? Was that it? 'Cheap date; buy some food for her and whisper sweet nothings into her ear and she'll get her kit off for you'?"

"Hell, no," I said firmly, "I don't think you understand how I feel about you."

"Then why do you have it?" she shouted.

"I was going to—"

"You were going to what? Work through the rest of the fucking book? God, you'll have no bedpost left at this rate, there must be hundreds of names in here. It'll be whittled down to a stick!" Her eyes widened as if she'd just realized something. "How do I even know what you said was true? That Isabella wasn't here last night because her name is in here? I bet you don't even have a stalker! I can't trust a single thing that comes out of your mouth!"

"Lucia, can you please let me explain? Let's go to breakfast or brunch. I don't care. Just anywhere so we can talk."

She looked at me, and I froze as I saw a tear roll down her cheek. Not tears! They made me feel helpless, wanting to give her the world to keep her from crying. Tears meant hurt, and I never meant to hurt her.

"I'm not going anywhere with you. I don't want to talk anymore, Jacob. I knew better than to date players, and I went against my gut," she finally said, hastily wiping away at her cheeks, as if her tears offended her. "You're no different, you're just another playboy player. I had hoped that you were something more, but, well, it doesn't matter now, does it?"

"Wait, it does matter," I said as she brushed past me and headed for the door. "Please don't do this. Wait a minute, Lucia, don't go!" I said louder, partially angry that she wasn't going to let me have my say and partially angry at myself for fucking up again. Hell, I needed her desperately and hadn't realized how much until this moment. I couldn't let her walk out of the house without an explanation. The problem was, if I told her the truth—everything, including the bet—she was going to fucking hate that explanation even more. I had been stupid, I had been childish, and I was about to lose the one thing that truly meant anything to me.

"I love you!" The words came out on their own accord. But I knew they were true the moment they touched the air. With a hopeful look I waited for her to say something, to turn back and hop into my arms, maybe. But instead more tears flowed and she turned away.

"Screw you, Jacob," she shouted as she exited the house, slamming the door behind her. I stopped in the foyer, unsure of what to do. What more could I say to convince her? The entire morning was supposed to be much better than this, but in the span of a few moments, I had just lost everything once more. And she had the book.

"Shit!" I yelled, screaming the word out into the empty house.

Chapter Twenty
LUCIA

I rushed to the car and climbed in, closed the door behind me and locked it before feeling foolish for doing just that. It wasn't like Jacob was going to pull the door off the hinges to stop me from leaving. I knew him well enough that he wasn't *that* type of guy...

Wait. Did he really say that he loved me? It didn't matter; he had hurt me again. The evidence of that was in the damp streaks on my face. In one last desperate attempt to see if he cared, truly cared, I glanced back at the front door. But he wasn't tearing down the steps following me. The door remained closed. He really didn't care about me. I was just a conquest, the "unfuckable" woman in the book whom he could use as evidence to prove himself to his teammates.

Starting the engine, I wiped the tears from my cheeks and drove away, wishing to God and everyone else that I had listened to my dad all those years ago and stuck to my rule. Then I wouldn't be in so much pain right now.

I remembered the conversation he and I had had when I was sixteen and was starting to gain attention and looks from the players. *"Don't ever date any of these guys,"* he had said with firm authority one day as we watched the team practice from his owner's suite. *"I mean it, Lucia. You probably think I'm overacting, trying to project my baby girl—and I know, I know, you aren't a baby anymore; you're turning into a young lady. But Lucia, they are not the type to settle down and raise a family. They will break your heart, and they won't even look back. You will wish that you'd never laid eyes on any of them. So, please, for me honey, stay away from them, okay?"*

I'd agreed, wanting to make him happy, wanting to erase that worry line from his face. *"Okay, Daddy."* At that he'd put his arm around me and pulled me into a sideways hug.

He'd been so right. I felt like my heart had been ripped from my chest and stomped on.

My phone rang and I picked it up, seeing Jacob's number come across the screen. I ignored it and threw it down on the seat, letting it ring until my voicemail picked it up. I was not going to talk to him anymore. There was nothing that he could say to make this any better. I had the proof in the back pocket of my jeans. I could get them all fired if I showed it to my dad, but I knew going down that road would be going too far—doing something like that wasn't me. I couldn't be responsible for all those players losing their jobs. No, instead I would destroy it somehow, 'cause no woman in it deserved to be subjected to something that crude and distasteful.

The words they'd used to describe me played over and over in my head as I drove aimlessly around. I wasn't untouchable or frigid, I was just careful with who I gave my heart to. I didn't mind a bit of flirting, and until Jacob, I had considered all those guys off limits. Mainly because of my promise to my father and my professional ethics. But obviously I'd been too cold, too distant, too "stuck up", and no one had even been brave enough to even approach me. Except Jacob.

I pulled up at a red light as my phone started ringing again. Grabbing it out of the seat, I pressed ignore and let it go to voicemail again. I wanted to chuck it out the window, but all of my contacts were in there, and I didn't want to lose them. Instead I scrolled until I found Jacob's contact information and deleted him from the list, feeling a small amount of satisfaction at doing so. I would start afresh and stay far away from players from now on.

* * *

"That asshole! To do that, eugh! That was low. And here I was pushing you into it—encouraging you to go to him," Cara said as she banged her fist upon the table.

I polished off the last bite of my waffle with a sigh and pushed the plate away. Instead of the breakfast-brunch I thought I was going to have with Jacob that morning, I ended up going home, making mulch out of the flowers that had stared at me from the coffee table, then crawling into bed and crying my eyes out until I had felt like I had gotten it all out of my system. Then Cara had called, demanded that I got out of bed, and decided that she was going to take me out instead. Though it was late afternoon, she'd found an all-day breakfast café that served waffles and bacon and had picked me up from the house.

As bravely as I could and without too many tears, I explained what had happened last night and this morning, even showing her the offending book that had ruined what had started out as a good day. She flipped through it and then threw it on the table, disgusted with what she had seen. "What are you going to do now? Maybe we should burn it. Or, even better, maybe you should give it to your father. That'll teach those sons of bitches!" she said with scorn.

"I don't know, but I won't do that," I said honestly, fiddling with a napkin to keep myself occupied.

"Yeah, you're probably right… karma would turn around and bite you on the ass instead."

"Eugh, but how can I show my face around work now considering all the players are not coming to my appointments? And now that I know about that *thing*, I don't want them to, either. They must all laugh at me behind my back. I'm so screwed."

"Have you given any thought to my offer?" she asked as the waitress brought our checks. "I found this perfect space near the coast that's relatively inexpensive, and it's in a great location. There are three offices, so if in the future we wanted to add another partner, we could. Plus there's an apartment above it that I was thinking of taking, too. And, that's not all… if you ever want to move out of that guest house, there's a spare room with your name on it."

I bit my lip, thinking of what I would have to do in order for that to happen. I would have to go to my father and talk about what wasn't working, admit that I was a failure even after he'd gone through all the trouble of creating the position for me. But at least the players and the coaches would be ecstatic to see me leave. "I don't know," I said slowly, looking at her.

"Come on, Lucia, this is the perfect time for a new start."

"But I would feel like a complete failure if I just walked away."

"You're not a failure, you're just re-evaluating your goals. You're not a failure unless you give up, and this won't be giving up. You'll be taking a new direction instead," Cara announced, reaching across the table to touch my arm. "Please, don't let one guy dictate the rest of your life. That goes for your father, too. If you want to stay at the stadium, then I will support you one hundred percent, but I worry that if you do, you'll be stuck in a toxic environment with nothing but failure in sight."

"Me too," I sighed, looking at the little black book as my stomach twisted nervously, nausea rising in my throat. I forced it down and took a sip of my water.

"Well, just think about it, but I think you are doing the right thing cutting this guy out of your life," Cara decided. "He's not worth your time or your effort. And I am so sorry that I even gave you any advice on him to start with."

I wanted to tell her that Jacob wasn't such a bad guy,

but the words would not form on my tongue. Maybe I was deluding myself. I had hoped that he was one of the good ones, the gem amongst the rocks, but I had been dead wrong. The nausea came back and I excused myself, rushing to the bathroom just in time to upchuck every morsel I had just eaten. Great. Now I was getting sick on top of everything else.

When I got back to the table, Cara was looking at me suspiciously. "Are you okay?" she asked. I nodded and grabbed my check, wanting to just go home and rest before the weekend was over. I was literally drained from everything that had happened. "Yeah I'm fine, just tired. Think I'm coming down with a bug, though."

"Okay, maybe we should get you some soup and fluids before I take you back home? Knowing you, you probably haven't shopped for weeks," Cara replied as she grabbed her check as well. We exited the booth and walked up to the register to pay. "I've been meaning to ask you, are you using a new moisturizer or bronzer? It looks really good—you've got a nice glow."

I gave her a wan smile, my heart pounding in my ears. I wasn't using anything new. A fleeting thought crossed my mind, and I dismissed it immediately. No, that couldn't be the case; me coming down with the flu and being sick combined with a facial glow didn't warrant *that* train of thought. Besides, I was on the pill, and we'd used protection… hadn't we?

Chapter Twenty One
JACOB

"**M**addox. Coach wants you in his office pronto."

I threw the shirt over my head and nodded at the assistant coach, fear welling up inside. It had been days since the fight with my father and the blow-up with Lucia. She wasn't returning any of my calls, and I'd already filled up her voicemail to the point where it wouldn't take any more. Every time I walked by her office, trying to act casual, the door was shut. I'd been too worried that she had a patient in there and hadn't knocked. It wasn't like I hadn't seen her, though. She had been on the sidelines during one of the practices with her father, talking and laughing like all was good in her world while I was in what seemed to be a state of limbo. Would she tell her father? She had evidence that could get me fired, and I wouldn't hold her against her if she went to him with the playbook and got us all thrown off the team.

And now the coach wanted to see me in his office. That was not a good sign.

I walked as slowly as I possibly could, almost dragging my feet as I went. I entered the large space that housed all the coaches' offices and passed a collection of desks, a bullpen of sorts with stacks of binders—no doubt filled with tactics and plays—piled up on every surface. I finally stood before the head coach's private office. I knocked on the glass panel of the closed door, and two men raised their heads. I felt like the floor was about to cave in underneath me as I saw David Cortes, the owner and Lucia's dad, seated at the desk beside Coach. Both their expressions were unreadable, blank as my paycheck would be after the meeting, I was sure of it.

I braced myself and entered the room as Coach gestured me in. What had Lucia told her father? Had she turned in the playbook? Were my dreams of becoming a starting quarterback again going to end right here? Damn Terrence and the rest of the guys.

"Jacob, sit down," the coach said, pointing to the other chair in the room. I swallowed hard as I sat.

Tiny beads of sweat prickled to the surface of my brow. I was about to lose everything—my career and the only woman that had truly given a damn about me.

"I'm sorry," I started, trying to head them off. Maybe if I could tell my side of things, they would reconsider firing my ass. "I can explain everything, I swear."

The coach looked at Mr. Cortes and then back at me. "What the hell are you talking about, son? Did you do something to Danny?"

"Danny?" I repeated, surprised. I had just seen Danny, our starting QB, only yesterday and his throws were as hot as ever. "What's wrong with Danny?"

"It's his shoulder. He tweaked his rotator cuff last night while lifting," Coach explained.

"Left or right?" I asked, the seriousness of the situation dawning on me.

"Right."

Fuck, that's his throwing arm.

"We're looking at four to six weeks recovery time if we're lucky," Coach continued. "He's getting checked out right now, and they don't think he's torn anything, but if he did, well, who knows? It could be eight weeks or more before he's tip-top again. And you're probably guessing why you're here now. We need you to step up to the plate, Jacob."

Suddenly, the room got extremely small as I realized this was my big break, a chance to regain some of my former glory. This was what I had been hoping to have happen, not that I wanted Danny to get hurt, that is. He was a cool guy with three kids at home, so he needed to work. But a minimum of four weeks on the field would give me enough time to show them what I had.

"This is very serious, Jacob," Mr. Cortes interjected. His features were hard to read, but his tone was stern—no nonsense. "I will not tolerate anything but stellar performances from my starters. One wrong move and you will be gone, you hear me? I don't care how much I spent on you."

"Y-yes, sir," I replied, wondering if he was actually referring to football, or something or someone else. "I will give you the best I got, that I can promise."

"See, Cortes, I told you he was ready." Coach grinned, giving me a nod. "I'll get Thomas to switch to Jacob, and I will work with him personally, too, get him up to speed. He'll catch on quick." Thomas was the quarterback coach, and we'd gotten along well since my arrival, but his time had always been primarily focused on Danny—as it should be, of course—but it was going to be good to get some proper attention from him.

"I won't let either of you down," I added as the owner rose from his chair.

"I need you focused, Jacob," Coach continued as Mr. Cortes stood by the door, his arms crossed over his chest. "You seem a little preoccupied lately. Can you shake that off? Anything we can help with?"

"No, there's no problem. Consider my head in the game," I answered. My now practically non-existent relationship with Lucia would need to take a back burner, even though I knew deep down I hadn't given up. It would just have to wait. Maybe it would be for the best anyway— give us both some time to cool off. After all, this was my career, my livelihood, and if I screwed this opportunity up, there certainly wouldn't be another one any time soon.

"One more thing," Coach said. "There's some guy calling the stadium, the offices, every number he can get a hold of, it seems, claiming he's your father and wanting his family ticket discount. I looked up his name and he's not on your list."

My jaw clenched. He was starting this shit again? I could see it now. It would be another repeat performance of his insane actions up in Minnesota. Fuck, it would just be like when I was a kid on my high school football team... I was going to kill the man. Why couldn't he just leave me alone and get on with his own life?

"Marshall Maddox is nothing to me," I replied evenly. "Don't give him anything."

"All right, I'll make a note of it," Coach said. Mr. Cortes eyed me carefully. He seemed to be attempting to read my mind; another moment passed without him saying anything.

"So, shall I go—"

"Jacob, if we need to get you some extra security for you, we can make that happen," Mr. Cortes interrupted. "Just let me, Greg here, or one of the security staff know, and we'll get it all set up. You shouldn't have to worry about these things."

I nodded, thinking it was pretty cool of him to offer. "Thanks. I'll let you know if it comes to that."

"Before I forget, this conversation is between us right now, Jacob," Coach added as I stood to go. "We'll make a formal announcement to the press about Danny's injury and you taking the number one spot before the game, but I don't want the press catching wind that you are the starter before then, okay?"

"Again, not a problem. My lips are sealed until you give the word," I replied, anxious and ready to prove myself. My day had just taken a turn for the better, and though the problems with Lucia were still heavy on my mind, this was good. I think she would be proud to know that I was going to get my chance.

"Good. See you on the field," he said, turning back to his paperwork. I walked past Lucia's father and out into the corridor, my mind already reeling through all the things I needed to work on and to prepare to fully take advantage of the opportunity.

"Jacob, a moment."

I turned and saw Mr. Cortes striding toward me, his stone-cold expression giving me pause. He sidled up to me and took my arm in a firm grip. "Stay the hell away from my daughter," he said, his voice low. It felt like a bucket of ice had been dropped on me.

"She told you?" I stammered. Why on earth would she do such a thing? Surely it would be bad for her, too?

His eyes blazed with a look of triumph and fury. "Does it really matter who told me?"

"No, I guess not. Oh, fuck," I muttered under my breath, but Mr. Cortes still heard it.

"Yeah, boy, you fucked up. I don't know what you did to her, but if I catch you near her again I will can you without question. You'll never play football again. Do you understand?"

"Yes," I replied, swallowing hard. Why on earth did she have to go tell him? No one else except Terrence knew, and he wasn't about to snitch on us; it was in his own best interest not to.

My arm throbbed as he released me. There would be some pretty hefty indentations from where his grip had been, I thought. He nodded, satisfied that he'd put the fear of God into me and resumed walking down the corridor to the field, leaving me standing there with my thumb up my ass.

Chapter Twenty Two
LUCIA

No.

Fuck, no.

I looked at the test again. My head became light and woozy as I sat on the toilet seat. My stomach rolled uncomfortably. After spending nearly three days and nights in bed feeling like I had been hit by a truck, I'd woken up that morning throwing up again. But that wasn't all; my breasts felt heavy and full. Though I was in complete denial of the fact that pregnancy could be a possibility—it just had to be the flu or some kind of virus, it had to be—I dragged myself to the local drugstore. I managed to avoid both Merry and my father on my little quest.

To make sure, I'd bought seven different types of tests. Now I had six of them all lined up on the bathroom counter, all telling me the same exact thing. I was pregnant. And it was Jacob's baby. *Shit.*

After placing the last test in line on the counter with the rest, I put my head in my hands. How could I have screwed up this badly? My period was slightly irregular, but I always remembered to take my pill to help with the irregularity. I never would have expected this to happen.

I remembered we'd used condoms once we'd started our marathon sex session inside the house, but that first time, in the pool, when I'd practically dangled myself in front of him, we'd used nothing. What had I been thinking? It was totally and completely out of character for me to be so irresponsible, to throw that much caution to the wind and gamble with my future. Well I had lost, big time. What was I going to do? There was no doubt in my mind that I was pregnant now. Hell, I had half a drug store on my counter saying as much!

Lifting my head, I moved just in time to throw up yet again. I retched; there was nothing at all left in my stomach to throw up.

My dad was going to kill me. Merry would be supportive of course, and so would Cara, but raising a child? Was I ready for that? I didn't have much experience with children and didn't really know the first thing about taking care of a baby. My life was in shambles—living in my parent's guest house, for fuck's sake—but in about eight short months I would be responsible for another living, breathing, and helpless human? I wasn't ready. Of course it wasn't the only option… there were alternative solutions, but touching upon each of them in my mind, I didn't think I could live with going through with any of them.

Touching my still flat stomach, I wondered what the baby would look like or how he or she would feel about me. What would Jacob say? Did I even want to tell him? He had a right to know, no matter what he'd done to me, I debated with myself.

Dropping my hand, I knew I had to tell him, given his past with his own father or the little bit I knew about it, anyway. It wouldn't be right to keep it to myself and deny him a chance of being a father. But could I let him back into my life after what he'd done? The thought of raising a child with someone who wasn't a partner left me feeling hollow. That was not how I'd envisaged it going. We might raise a child together, but the hurt of how it had happened still burned a hole in my chest. With a sigh, I eased myself up and walked out of the bathroom to my closet to get ready for work. I'd taken too much time off. Any more and it would become suspicious.

* * *

I rose out of my seat carefully as the knock became insistent on my office door. I wondered who on earth was trying to beat it down. Every day I closeted myself in the space, no longer leaving the door open or ajar. I didn't want to run the risk of having Jacob barge in here and demand I listen to whatever excuse he was going to rattle off. But after three knocks, I felt like I should answer it. It might not be him but someone who really needed some help, and I couldn't pretend not to be in.

Opening the door, I took one look at his face and shut it again, locking it for good measure. "Go away."

"What the hell did you tell your father, Lucia?" he asked, his voice muffled through the wood. Tell my father? I hadn't told him anything about Jacob and our undefinable relationship. And I surely had not said one word about the baby growing inside me. He would have a fit if that little tidbit was just blurted out, but I knew I couldn't hide it forever. I'd have Merry there with me when I finally had to break the news, though.

"He's riding my ass, telling me to stay away from you," he continued. "Hell, Lucia, he's going to make my life miserable."

"So what do you want me to do about it?"

"I dunno," he said, exasperated. "Open the door—we really need to talk, unless you want everyone to hear our business. I'm so sorry, truly I am. You believed me once before, believe me now when I say that book you found, it doesn't mean anything. It only led me to you. My feelings are real, Lucia."

I leaned my forehead against the cool wood and willed myself to stay strong. I could not allow myself to fall back on my word now. Plus, today was not a good day to tell Jacob about the possibility of a baby. I still needed to get a doctor to confirm that it was real and had made an early appointment the next day. "Just go away, Jacob, please," I pleaded, feeling the nausea roll in my stomach.

"Eugh! But why tell your father? I can't believe you would do such a thing," he continued, as if I hadn't even spoken. I hadn't done anything—I was too wrapped up in the newest issue in my life to even think about telling my father about our sexcapades. He was going to totally ignore that fact anyway when he found out about the baby. No, I had bigger issues than Jacob's insecurities about his job. He should have thought about that before he cracked open that stupid book.

"It doesn't matter now anyway. It's not like you didn't deserve a reaming," I shot back, hurt in my voice. "Clearly I was just a conquest for you and your stupid black book. So why don't you just leave me alone?"

"Oh, come on, Lucia," he answered roughly. "You never let me explain that. What we have, it's more than that."

I couldn't help but choke back laughter, thinking that he was right on that account. What we had could've been so much more if he hadn't turned into a huge jerk-face. Jacob jiggled the door handle, and I paused, another wave of nausea nearly overpowering me. I gagged as I ran to my trash can, upchucking the few crackers I'd eaten this morning.

"Lucia?" Jacob asked. "Shit. Are you okay?"

"Go away," I forced out, wiping my mouth with a tissue I grabbed from the box on my desk. If this was real and I was pregnant, I didn't want anything to do with it; the nausea was almost constant now, and I felt miserable. I probably looked miserable, too, and all I wanted was to be left alone. The door jiggled harder, and I froze, prying my fingers away from the edge of the trash can. I couldn't let him in. Reaching over,

I picked up my office phone and speed-dialed security.

"Security. How may we assist you?"

"Um, yes, I think someone has just hit a car in the parking lot," I said in an almost whisper so Jacob wouldn't overhear me. "I think it's Jacob Maddox' car. You might want to call him and tell him. They're driving off. Oh my God, he's going to be so pissed!" I hung up immediately as the guard started to ask more questions. It wasn't long before I heard Jacob's phone ring on the other side of the door.

"Yeah? What? Shit, I will be there in a moment. Lucia, this is not over with yet, not by a long shot."

I heard his footsteps recede down the hall and sighed in relief, glad that I was able to get him away from the door. I needed to figure all of this out first before I told anyone about the baby. Hell, I didn't even believe it myself and needed someone official to tell me it was happening, not just take the word of some pee on a few plastic sticks.

But though it was scary as hell, even I had to admit, partially exciting, too. I was potentially going to be a mother, giving my father and Merry their first grandchild. So what if the father was not going to be involved? I could provide for this child, but I couldn't stay here anymore. It had become abundantly clear that I needed to quit, start new like Cara had said, and move on to something where my skills and help would be appreciated and not belittled.

With the decision made I picked up my phone, scrolled to Cara's number and texted her, asking if she could meet for lunch. I wanted to see this office space.

* * *

The next day Cara and the realtor followed not far behind me as I walked through the quirky rooms of the empty office. Cara was right, the location was fantastic. Set in a converted townhouse, it was a stone's throw from the ocean but close enough to everything that we would ever need. Plus it had a small parking lot around back for clients.

On the ground floor, the actual working spaces, the offices, were very spacious but still had a good homely feel about them, perfect for therapy sessions. I could imagine my diplomas on the walls and a nice desk in the corner with the picture windows behind me. I knew I could work well in this environment. The whole building gave off a good tranquil vibe, even the apartment upstairs which Cara was eager to show me, was gorgeous.

"Well?" Cara asked as I turned to face them. "What do you think?"

"It's perfect," I said, the first real smile on my face in quite a number of days.

"So, what does that mean exactly?" Cara prodded, not quite happy with my elusive answer. "Are you going to come in with me? You know we'll be great at it. It's what we always talked about in college."

"It's a big step," I said slowly. "My father is going to hit the roof when he hears I want to leave." I had such high hopes for that job, but the writing was definitely on the wall. I couldn't stay. If I did, I was going to have the life sucked out of me with no support from the coaching staff. Twiddling my thumbs was not my idea of trying to make a difference. I wanted to help people.

"Take your dad out of the picture for just a moment, Lucia," Cara said, putting her hands on her hips. "What do you want to do? What would make you happy?"

I looked around the empty office and thought about it. What *would* make me happy? The list was short, barely a list at all—this was on it and so was one annoying quarterback. I smiled. "I want this. Let's do it."

"Yes!" Cara exclaimed, walking over to hug me.

"We are so going to kick ass! I had all kinds of ideas for advertisements, too. Word will spread, Lucia, and they'll flock to us."

I grinned at her enthusiasm, hoping that I wouldn't let her down, too. I also hoped that some of her excitement would rub off on me. Right now I was too preoccupied thinking about the baby growing inside me. My early morning appointment had confirmed that I was indeed up the duff. I hadn't even told Cara, not yet knowing how I truly felt. She would be totally supportive, that I had no doubt about, but there was still something inside me, an instinct of sorts to just keep the information to myself a little while longer. Like I needed to fully digest what was happening to me. I guessed I had to let it sink in properly before I was ready to hear anyone else's opinion on the matter.

I would have to come up with some way of breaking the news to Jacob soon, though. That I couldn't chicken out on. But I did think telling Jacob was probably going to be a lot easier than telling my father. The moment my father found out that a player had defiled his precious daughter, World War Three would start.

"You okay, Luce?" Cara asked, picking up on my quietness. I should've been jumping up and down, ecstatic about this new venture, and in a way I was, I just had a hard time showing it right then.

"Yeah, don't you worry about me, I'm fine. Just nervous, I guess. But we're in this together, right?"

"Right!" She beamed at me, I loved seeing her happy.

Looking at my watch, I realized it was later than I'd thought. "I have to get to work—figure out how I'm going to quit and tell my father about all this," I said, looking at Cara. "Just send me the paperwork, okay? And I'll phone you later so we can start planning."

"I'm so excited!" she announced, giving me another hug. "This is going to be epic!"

I nodded and walked out of the townhouse, biting my lip as I went. I sure hoped so. Something in my life had to go right.

Chapter Twenty Three
JACOB

She had duped me. That sneaky little... I was impressed nonetheless. There was no one else that would have wanted me to come to the parking lot in such a hurry other than Lucia. After examining my car to ensure that nothing had happened to it, I'd gone over to the security office and found out after some prodding that the call had been anonymous. The security guy couldn't remember what number or extension it had come in on, so there was no way to find out who'd actually called. But I was ninety-nine percent sure I knew who had done it. And the next time I saw her, I was determined to confront her for real this time. A door wouldn't get in my way a second time.

A few days later I rounded the corner of the training building to see Lucia standing near the parking entrance by the gate. Her hands flew all about her, gesticulating wildly as she talked with someone in front of her.

God she was gorgeous, even hotter than I remembered, dressed in those prim white dress pants and a blue sleeveless shirt that showed off her toned arms. Despite my disappointment that she'd blabbed our business to her father, I still couldn't shake the feeling of needing her. So she wanted to play games? Well I was about to ruin her conversation and have a little fun myself.

Walking toward her, my grin slipped as I recognized the man she was arguing with. A scumbag I knew all too well. My pace quickened.

"You are not welcome here," Lucia was saying as I approached, her face red with anger. "I think you have done enough damage in his life, and he does not need someone like you harassing him."

"I don't know who you think you are, bitch," Marshall replied, stepping closer to Lucia, a menacing look in his eye. I broke into a run; I'd seen that look too many times. I knew what came next. "But I don't take too kindly to people telling me what to do, especially a woman."

Before the worst could happen I was between them.

"I told you to leave me the hell alone," I said and spotted the look of surprise on Lucia's face. "Get out before I call security."

My father edged closer to me. My words seemingly had no effect—but I knew that already. The only thing Marshall understood was violence. Lucia chose that moment to reinsert herself, angering him even further.

"Just leave! you're not wanted here," she said firmly. God, she had balls, and it made me love her even more.

But before I could stop him—too distracted admiring her strength—he pushed her away. She stumbled back, her heels giving way, and she fell over the curb, landing in the cut grass.

Immediately, I saw red and launched myself at him, knocking him to the ground hard, letting my fists do the talking. They planted themselves, blow after blow, into his leering face. His knee connected with my midsection, and the wind was momentarily knocked out of me, giving him the upper hand in the fight. I felt the sting of his punch as he connected with my cheek.

"You bastard," he seethed, spit flying out of his mouth as I tried to block his punch. "You think you are the big man now? Huh? You're not. You've never been nothing but a two-bit has-been and always will be."

The long buried rage that I'd managed to keep under control throughout all the years of abuse, violence and name-calling finally erupted. It burst through the surface as if a pressure valve had been released, and I flipped him. My fists pummeled his head and face.

Flesh tore and bones crunched as my onslaught raged. I couldn't make myself stop. "This is for all those times you said I wasn't good enough! This is for every beating you gave me for dropping the ball, for losing a game! This is for the hell you put me through as a child, you worthless piece of shit!" I shouted, the words coming out alongside heavy breaths. "And this," I said winding my arm back high, "is for daring to touch something that is mine!"

"Jacob! Stop it!" I felt the pull of someone on my shoulders and shrugged it off, wanting to kill the man under me. Another arm grabbed me, and I was dragged away from the bloodied man. My arms were pinned behind me, secured by faceless men I couldn't see because my sights were set on my target a few yards away. Marshall scrambled away and I launched at him again, but it was no use. I was hauled back by men a lot stronger than me. Terrence's worried face came into my view, trying to pull my focus to him. "Hey, dude, it's me. You need to breathe. Calm down, okay?"

"I'm gonna kill him," I forced out, spitting blood onto the pavement and struggling against the men holding me. "Let me go!"

"Dude, you ain't going nowhere. Trey and Eddie won't let that happen," he said.

Behind me a voice added, "Too right I won't. Keep still… don't make me sit on you. You won't like that one bit." I recognized Trey's deep baritone and did as he asked for fear he'd made good on his promise to squash me like a bug if I didn't stop struggling.

Lucia hovered into view. "Please, Jacob," she begged, "he's not worth it."

I drew in a painful breath, my eyes focusing on her gorgeous face. Just looking at her soothed me, but panic soon filtered through as I remembered Marshall pushing her to the ground. "Are you okay? He didn't hurt you, did he?"

"I-I'm fine," she said with a small smile. "I'm fine, and you will be, as well."

"Guys, you can let go now, I'm okay. I promise I won't do anything."

After a moment, Terrence nodded to Trey and Eddie behind me, and their hands finally fell away, releasing me. I looked around. Half the team had spilled out of the locker room, all of them giving me wary looks. The press, along with their cameras—ready for an open practice day— were also there, still on the other side of the gate but close enough to have witnessed at least some of the fight.

"Maddox!" Coach barked as he came over. I was expecting to see anger evident on his face, but there was only concern. "Showers. Now. Go cool off!" I started to open my mouth, but he shook his head and looked at Lucia. "Get him the hell out of here, Lucia. This is going to be a shit-storm like no other."

"Come on, Jacob," she whispered, laying her hand on my arm. I looked down, seeing the reddened scratches from where she had fallen on her forearm, and I growled, wanting to start round two with the person who called himself my father. He had hurt her, and it was my fault.

She sensed my anger building, and for a second she squeezed my arm, forcing me to look into her eyes. "Please, let's go. Don't let him get the best of you, Jacob."

I took in another breath and nodded. The rush of adrenaline was starting to fade away, only to be replaced with the small beginnings of pain from where he'd hit me. It was a familiar pain, one that I hadn't felt in a long time. It was different to the hits I'd experienced on the field; these were full of malice and hatred. And it felt like they hit me harder, like they didn't just wound me physically.

Lucia gave me a small smile, and together we walked into the locker room. She steered me toward the showers and entered the room, pushing the door closed behind her. "Come on," she said as she locked the door and stepped forward. "Let's get you cleaned up first."

"I'm so damn sorry, Lucia, for everything," I forced out as she reached for the hem of my jersey. She bit her lip, her fingers mere inches away from the skin on my hip. "Shh, let's talk about it in a little while, okay?"

I surrendered to her, allowing her to pull the shirt over my head. "You are going to be so sore tomorrow," she said absently, touching the middle of my abdomen with her gentle fingers. I grimaced as she touched the tender spot, feeling my own desire rise at her soft touch. God, I needed her so badly it hurt. I was in pain in more ways than one.

She stepped aside and turned on the water. The steady stream of the hot spray splashed on the tiles, and she looked back at me. I couldn't stand the look of pity in her eyes and forced my shorts down over my hips, stepping angrily out of my shoes. I had done it again. I had allowed my personal business to interfere with my profession.

I would be lucky to still have a spot on the team after all this went down! When was my life ever going to be damn normal?

Stepping under the water, I was fully aware of Lucia watching my every move, as if I might to lose it at any moment, but having her there kept me on a relative even keel. The hot water scalded my scrapes and the bruises that had begun to form, and I welcomed the dull, throbbing pain. I deserved to hurt after what I'd done. Embarrassing myself in front of her and practically the entire team. Not to mention the rest of the world, if the press had their way.

When her hands touched my back, I shivered. I felt dirty, worthless—I wasn't the man for her. She was a therapist, successful and gorgeous, for Christ's sake, and I was, well, I was a fucking screw-up. Always had been, always will be, just like the man had said. He'd said it all my life; it was a wonder I was only realizing it now. Her arms encircled my waist, and I held my breath, the steam of the water starting to fog up around us.

"It's not your fault," she said softly, kissing the middle of my back. "Everything will be okay, Jacob."

I turned around quickly and pulled her against me, feeling her wet, naked body against mine.

My cock jumped to attention. I hadn't heard or noticed her getting undressed, but here she was, bare before me again. Wanting me. Perhaps I wasn't so worthless after all.

"Can we save the therapy session for later?" I asked, bending my head. "I need something else."

She nodded and I captured her lips with mine, taking no prisoners as I plundered her mouth with my tongue. Her hands gripped my back tightly as I cupped her bare ass and walked us both back to the half wall that separated the stalls, forcing her to sit on it. I tore myself from the kiss and rested my forehead against hers. Our breathing was harsh and echoed all around us. "You're everything that's good in my life, you know that?" I said, gripping her hips. "I need you like I need the air I breathe, and I am going to have you. Hard and without any regret. Are you okay with that?"

"Yes, I need you, too," she panted, wrapping her long legs around my waist. She was taking a huge risk being in here, let alone being naked in here and wanting me to fuck her, but I wasn't going to think about that now. I growled and pulled her to me, pushing into her wet entrance with one deep thrust. She gasped, and I held still, allowing her to adjust to my length before I started to move rapidly within her.

I hadn't been bluffing. I took her like the world was ending and we had only seconds to live. Our bodies crashed together, each taking what we needed from each other without mercy.

Her fingernails raked my back, pleasurably digging into my skin. The tang of her natural scent rising from her sex made my head dizzy as I dipped my head lower, down to her breasts. She tasted sweet, better than I remembered. A vague hint of vanilla and salt coated my tongue as I licked and nibbled my way around the swollen nub. Her legs clamped around me harder, and she threw her head back. Seeing her exposed like that, her torso stretched out and her tits circling upon her chest, made me pound into her harder.

She let out a cry that mingled with the word *yes*, which only made me go faster.

As the first orgasm overcame her, her throaty moans bounced and clashed off the tiles of the room so that it almost sounded like there was a whole orgy going on in there. Thrusting faster, I took all of her weight, held onto the cheeks of her bum, swung her body away and then back towards me over and over again, my cock sliding roughly in and out of her delicious, tight cunt. All the frustration of the days and weeks without her melted away with every passing second that I was buried within her.

But it would be over too soon.

As she bit her lip, the walls of her pussy clenching furiously around my shaft, a sign that she was on the brink of another orgasm, I slipped the tip of my finger slowly into her virgin ass. Her eyes grew wide, momentarily shocked, but then her mouth dropped open and out came a euphoric moan. The sound of her enjoying herself was the biggest turn on ever. I felt the hot rush of her juices coating the head of my cock, and I came hard and fast, shouting as I poured into her, unleashing everything I had.

Chapter Twenty Four
LUCIA

'd just had sex in the team shower. That had to be a first for a lot of people, though I was sure many cheerleaders had seen the inside of the room. It had also been the first time anyone had ever done *that* to me, too. I blushed as I remembered, but God, did it feel good. I was experiencing a lot of firsts today, I thought.

Jacob was still gripping my hips tightly, as I too was still clinging to him, my arms around his neck. The intensity of his stare as we recovered in each other's embrace was like nothing I'd experienced before. I wanted to tell him everything that I was feeling right then but was too scared to even form the words, too scared to break the perfect moment.

My legs started to ache, and I thought I would no doubt be feeling the burn of our workout for some days to come. But for some reason, I couldn't find the bad in it. The look on Jacob's face as he had stood under the shower had almost broken my heart, and before my conscience could kick in, I had stripped off my clothes (again—seriously, what was it about Jacob Maddox that made me want to get naked all the time?) and gone in to comfort him.

Cramp started to set in, and I began shivering—the aftershocks of what seemed like an endurance session taking its toll on my barely used muscles. I forced my legs to lose their grip on Jacob's waist, and he stepped away. The smell of sex mingled in the air with the steam, even though the water was still running. I stood, a bit wobbly, and reached for one of the towels on the cart just outside the shower. We didn't say a word as we went through the motions of getting dry. I toweled off briskly, needing to get back into my clothes before anyone decided to come find us. I heard him cut off the shower and grab a towel himself, the silence deafening now. I didn't know what to say, and my heart thudded in my chest. What did this mean for us now? Could I forgive him for what he'd done? Were the three little words he'd said, oh what seemed so long ago now, true?

"Lucia."

I looked up to find him studying me. There was a towel clinging low on his hips. I had forgotten how well-formed his body was, and my mouth went dry at the sight, my hands wanting to touch him again. My body wanted to shed my clothes again. I couldn't deny it any longer—I was head over heels for him. It didn't matter what career he had, he was the object of my affections, the father of my child, and that wasn't going to change. Of course the anger and hurt he'd caused me still lingered, but I knew I could give him a second chance. He deserved at least that. I could see he was hurting, too. His own buried troubles were coming to the surface. I had to be careful if I broached the subject; there was something nasty between him and his father, an unresolved and unhealed wound that had been niggling at him all these years, like a splinter that had dug itself a cozy home, festering beneath the surface. We would talk about it, if he wanted to, but not yet. Now he needed hope, needed to see there was a future for him.

"I'm pregnant," I blurted out, keeping my fingers crossed that this was the right time to tell him.

His eyes widened, and he stumbled back as if an invisible hand had slapped him. He said nothing, and I fumbled with the still-open buttons on my shirt, looking down and away from him. If he wasn't going to be happy, I didn't think I'd be able to look at him again.

All of a sudden his hands covered my own, stopping me from completing my task and forcing me to look up at him. His eyes were blazing, full of questions, and his throat was working hard. "You're pregnant?"

"A few weeks, yes," I answered as he gripped my wrists gently. "Seven positive home tests, all the signs, and one doctor's confirmation."

"Seven tests?" he asked, arching a brow. "What were you trying to prove?"

"It's not every day that you need to prove something so important," I said, dying to know what he was thinking. He grinned then, and I felt some of the worry of how he might react to the news slip away. Maybe, just maybe, this wasn't going to be a bad thing after all. "A baby?"

"As far as I can tell," I joked as he brought one of my wrists up and kissed it softly, sending a spiral of heat down to the center of my body. "Unless you are half alien or something?"

"Wow," he answered as his arm slipped around my waist. I felt my own body react to being pressed up against his naked one and tried without success to dampen down my hormones.

Wasn't there something about craving sex while pregnant? If so, I was in for some fun over the next few months or so. "I'm going to be a father? Oh wow, I'm going to be a dad," he said, the happy realization of what it all entailed finally hitting him.

His words nearly caused me to burst into tears, the wonderment of the way he spoke them so reverently erased any doubt in my mind that Jacob wanted to be involved in this child's life. "Yes," I said softly, winding my arms around his neck. "You are going to be a daddy."

He brushed a kiss over my lips before stepping back and grabbing his clothes off of the floor, looking a bit confused. "I... we need to go somewhere and talk, Lucia. About everything."

"Okay," I said, the moment gone for now. The wonder on his face was replaced with a serious expression, set and determined. "We can go to my office. We'll have privacy there."

"No," Jacob said sharply. "I-I need to get away from here. Somewhere with alcohol. We can talk and celebrate at the same time."

I couldn't help but smirk and slid my feet into my heels, looking down at his state of clothing. "Well, hurry up and get dressed then."

"Oh right, yes, that would help wouldn't it?"

he said with a sweet laugh. It was good to hear him like that, a little more relaxed even with the bombshell I'd just drop on him.

Jacob dressed quickly, and I flipped the lock on the shower before leading him out a back entrance used for laundry deliveries, where no one would be expecting us to be. Instead of trying to find my car, I hailed a cab and we climbed in. I gave the cab driver my address. It was risky to go home, but it was far too early to go to a bar. And given the nature of what had just transpired at the stadium, my father would be tied up with the press for hours. Merry would also be out of the picture. She was away visiting a friend for a few days, helping her to redecorate, too, so the guest house would be safe for the moment.

Jacob's hand found its way onto my thigh. He caressed it absently while he stared out the window during the drive. I let him be with his own thoughts, knowing he needed time to process everything. We arrived about ten minutes later, and I reached into my purse for my key card.

"This is your father's house?" Jacob said as the gate opened and I started to walk up the drive. The huge mansion loomed in the distance. "I can't be here, Lucia."

"It's a good thing that we aren't planning on going there then," I remarked and took his hand, leading him along the well-worn path to the guest house. I pushed open the door and stepped into the cool interior, waiting on Jacob to follow me. Finally he took a brave step inside. "Welcome to my little domain."

He looked around as I went to grab a beer and one bottle of water from the fridge. I never did have much food, but I always made sure that I was stocked up on beer at least. He accepted it gratefully, and I took a seat in my favorite overstuffed chair, watching as Jacob sat on the couch and popped open the beer. "Ah," he said after his first sip, "that's better. Tastes good."

"More in the fridge if you want," I said with a shrug. "'Cause I won't be drinking for a while."

He looked at me, a grin spreading across his face. "Oh, right, yeah. So are we really doing this?"

"Yes," I answered, my hand straying protectively to my stomach. "Not that I had planned on having a child now, but I've gone over it every which way from Sunday, and this is the right way for me. Don't ask me to—"

"That's not what I meant," he replied hastily, his eyes widening. "I mean, you are going to let me do this with you, right? You aren't going to tell me to take a hike because of what happened before, 'cause I really, really want to be part of this, Lucia. You and the baby."

I caught his drift, flushed, and skirted past it. "I would never deny you your right to be a father."

He nodded and sat back on the couch, taking another long sip of his beer. "I guess you are wondering what happened between me and my own father?"

I sat forward, hoping he'd see the sincerity in my eyes. "You don't have to tell me anything you don't want to. But I'm here to listen... not as a therapist, either, as a friend," I said.

Chapter Twenty Five
JACOB

She wanted to listen. I wasn't surprised at all, but it did feel nice that someone actually wanted to listen to me, to hear about my past. After all these years no one had ever taken the time to ask me if everything was okay at home—not my teachers, nor my friends' parents, no one. So, why couldn't it be the mother of my child? I smiled a little then, taking in the word. Lucia was to be a mom, and I was going to be a fucking dad. I thought this day would be years down the line. I never thought of myself settling down or even bringing a kid into the world, but the moment she'd told me, my heart had decided this was what I wanted. The news couldn't have come at a better time. Was I ready? Hell no. The thought of having someone who would look up to me, who would push me to do my damn best for them, that made my boots quiver with fear, but it still meant more than anything.

I looked down at the beer in my hand, bringing my thoughts back to the present. Lucia cleared her throat then took a sip of her water. She was beautiful and patient, and I didn't deserve her... "You want the Cliff Notes? Or the full version?"

She joined me on the sofa then and slipped a warm comforting hand into mine. "Whatever you want to tell me."

"God, where do I even start?" I said, mainly to myself. Was there even a beginning to the story that had become my miserable life? I supposed there was, but perhaps I was too young to realize it at the time.

I took a breath a let it all pour out. "My mom died in a car accident when I was five. I overheard the officers telling my father that she hadn't felt a thing, that it was quick. But I wasn't sure I believed them. The horrified looks on their faces as they stood on the doorstop told the five-year-old me that they were lying. Thinking back about it now, they probably always did that—to lessen the grief for those loved ones they had to visit. What made it worse, though, was I was supposed to be in that car with her."

"How so?"

"She'd come to collect me from a friend's house, but she hadn't turned up on time—three guesses as to why. She'd probably responded in a tone my father hadn't liked or forgotten to buy enough beer. It would've been something inane, but regardless, he would've beaten her for it.

"I'd waited for a little while, the time passing without my realizing it as I played with my friend. But it wasn't like Mom to forget. We had a routine, you see; she'd pick me up every Wednesday from Charlie's and just the two of us, we'd go run some errands—sneaking in a stop at the Double Scoop for ice cream. My dad never knew anything about it. It was our little secret, and he just thought we'd gone shopping. So when it started to get dark, and Charlie's mom started to put their dinner out, I got worried. It wasn't far from our own house, so I just walked home. I think we must've missed each other on the street. When I got home, Dad was passed out on the couch, his arm and bloodied fist dangling off the side, almost lifeless. And Mom was nowhere to be found. I checked everywhere, but the only thing I found was a small pool of still wet blood with a few drips trailing away from it in the kitchen."

Lucia squeezed my hand, and I suddenly realized I was crying. I sniffed the tears away and continued.

"As I got older and ran the memories back over and over in my mind, I started to piece things together, my theory being he'd hit her so hard that she must've bumped her head. I dunno, maybe he gave her concussion or something, and when she got in the car to come get me… well, yeah, she obviously wouldn't have been in any state to drive. Of course, I couldn't prove any of this—it was too late, anyway. Far too late. I wondered many times why she stayed, why she didn't leave him. If we'd left just one day earlier, she'd still be alive."

I took a deep breath, finding a shard of hurt still twisting within me, a dagger piercing my heart. I barely remembered my mom, but the pain never went away.

"Before my grandma died, she made sure that I knew what kind of man my father was and how much her daughter had suffered at his hands—like I didn't already know. He'd turned his attention to me, you see. 'He will get his someday,' she wheezed, still smoking a cigarette even though the cancer had eaten its way through her lungs. 'You just be patient and wait, Jacob. Don't show him any piece of you that is scared, or he will take full advantage of it. Suck it up and be a man, and as soon as you can, you leave, 'cause they'll make you go back with him. You hear me?'

"She died a few days later and I found out that she had been right about not having anywhere else to go. I was a burden to him," I said, clenching my hand tightly around the bottle. "A constant reminder of my mom and what he had done. And since she wasn't around for him to beat on, he turned to me. I had my first black eye at six."

"Oh my God," Lucia breathed, "why didn't anyone do anything about that?"

I gave her a sharp laugh, shaking my head. "Not for a snot-nosed kid from the wrong side of the tracks. No one gave a shit. They all had their own problems." I didn't want to look at Lucia. I didn't want to see the pity in her eyes. "So when I was old enough, I signed up for anything that would keep me from having to go home." I told her how I had no money of my own—what kid does? And I wasn't able to get a job until my mid-teens, but my grandma's words stuck in my head. I had to get out and away from him. Luckily I was still able to do a ton of things to keep out of his way— baseball, football, anything sports-related, really. I can still remember my first coach, Eric Danes, and how he had taken a shine to me, inviting me over to eat when he knew I hadn't had a proper meal in days. His house had been so different from my own—even the atmosphere, you know, was lighter. There had been nights I wanted to be his son and live in his house."

"What did your father think of your decisions?" she asked softly. I cleared my throat and took another swallow of beer. "He liked it, actually. He pushed me to excel at any and all sports. The only problem was when I didn't do my 'best' or let him down. He was careful to hit me where no one else would notice. I've had cracked ribs more times than I care to admit.

"I played both baseball and football through middle school until I won the quarterback position on the varsity team in my first year of high school. My father got wind of it and forced me to concentrate on football, stating that my money chances were higher there. He was always talking about how I'd take care of him—how I'd pay him back once I made it big. It was like I owed him just for existing, for being unfortunate to have been spawned from him. He was ruthless and ten times worse than any of my coaches. There were many nights when he forced me to throw spiral after spiral though a tire he'd rigged up in our backyard. I had to do it so many times in a row before I was allowed to stop. And the numbers just kept climbing. First it would be ten times in a row, then twenty, then fifty. Sometimes, I could barely move my throwing arm the next morning as a result.

"When did the beatings stop?" Lucia asked.

I looked at her, her expression full of compassion. "They didn't, not really. The frequency dropped when I was old enough and big enough to fight back, and that was around my junior year. I'd thrown an interception in an important game, causing it to be a lot closer than it should've been. And though we won, my father made sure I would never forget the mistake I'd made."

"You worthless excuse for a son!" he raged, pushing me against the wall hard, his hand wrapped around my throat. I could see the whites of his eyes, his spittle raining down on my face as my head banged against the wall. "You almost blew our chance at greatness!"

"Our chance?" I asked, feeling the rage build up, swelling like an unstoppable storm. "There is no 'our'! This has nothing to do with you!"

"You ass-wipe," he said as I fought against the hand at my throat. "I have clothed and fed your miserable behind for years. You owe me, and don't you EVER forget that."

He released me then, laughing as I crumbled to the floor in a fit of coughs. "You're a little piss-ant, weak as a twelve-year-old girl, but I will make you strong so you don't throw like shit again. I'll beat it into you if I have to." He lifted his boot to kick me, but I got there first. My foot shot out, stopping him, pushing him on his ass across the living room floor.

"Of course, it just pissed him off more, but I was

able to escape and walked the three miles to my coach's house, and he took me in without a word. I suspect he knew about the beatings all along but never said anything because I never did.

"He'd still come to my games though, and stand glaring at me the whole time. He never cheered—unless you counted him calling me every name under the sun, like he was on the opposing team. It was as if he was daring me to make a mistake. Maybe he wanted me to make one so I would somehow get kicked off the team and have to come crawling back to him. And though his acts of intimidation did get to me somewhat, I muddled through. When the college scholarships started to pour in, he backed off a little," I continued, remembering those days well. "I was so excited that I was finally going to get away from him for good, free to do whatever I pleased."

"I can only imagine the relief you must've felt," Lucia said as she tucked her feet under herself and snuggled in close to my side. Absently I stroked her hair as the words continued to fall out; the dam had broken.

"Yeah, I couldn't wait. I took the offer that was as far away from home as possible, and for a kid who had never tasted any freedom whatsoever, my first year was nearly a disaster. Had it not been for the coaching staff riding my ass to bring up my grades, I would have flunked out. But in my third year, I broke nearly every record the school had," I said, remembering the winning feeling, the high that could not be broken. "Scouts were showing up left and right to watch me play, and the bets were already starting to be laid as to where I would end up. I was getting all the sex I wanted, too, night after night." Realizing what had just slipped out, I sheepishly looked up at Lucia. "Sorry, babe."

She gave me a warm smile, her hand straying to her stomach. "I don't mind your past; it's made you who you are today. You've been through a lot—a lot more than any kid should have to go through, and really, the only thing that matters now is our, I mean your future." I swallowed hard, my eyes drifting to her well-placed hand. Hell yeah, that was all that mattered now. I was going to be the best fucking father any child could ever have. But it wasn't just that. The woman who was listening to me, I would crawl a thousand miles to get her forgiveness. I would never feel worthy enough to be with her. She deserved a hell of a lot better than me.

"In one respect, I thought you were a typical jock, but on the other hand you were also a bit of a mystery, if I'm being honest. I'm so glad you told me about what happened with you and your dad. It makes me feel closer to you."

"Me, too. I feel lighter somehow." I threaded my fingers through hers and wondered what I'd done to meet someone like her.

"So what happened next, you know, after all the sex?" she asked, gently teasing me.

"Oh, you want to hear more?"

"Of course I do."

"Okay then. After that, with all the scouts sniffing around, the coach told me that I could go into the draft. He didn't want me to, but hell, that was my dream, the thing I had been working toward all my life. I met with an agent and dropped out of the school the next day."

Looking back, I was an idiot to do so. Another year and I would have graduated with a degree in public relations, something that I could have used when or if my football career tanked. It's the one mistake all college athletes make, thinking they are invincible enough to play for twenty or so years. "Anyway," I continued, shaking off that mood, "when the draft came, I went in the first round. You probably know some of this. But the money, hell, it was more than I could have ever imagined. After all my struggles growing up, barely having enough to eat 'cause it all went to feeding my father's beer and whiskey habit, I saw it as an opportunity to make my own way in life without the shadow of my father hanging over me. I spent and wasted far too much, but it was worth it. And the first few games, I rocked it. But then the phone calls started, and the visits. He was in my head all the damn time, making me lose focus. And then…"

"Then something happened?" she asked, and my mood darkened immediately. I sighed and dropped my head, wishing I could go back to that one game that changed my damn life forever.

"Maddox! Suit up! You're going in!"

Pumped, I grabbed my helmet and slammed it onto my head, trotting out onto the field to the roar of the crowd. The game that was going to push us into the playoffs hung in the balance, the team down by a touchdown with less than a minute left on the clock. I'd been benched for throwing an interception a week earlier, but now was my time to bring the glory back. If I could pull this off, we were going to be in the playoffs, which meant a bonus was coming my way.

I huddled with the offense and rattled off the play call, clapping my hands to break the huddle before positioning myself behind the center. It was an easy route, a fake to my running back before an easy throw downfield to my open receiver. I had done it a thousand times before. I did a hard count and backed up, faking the handoff and setting up my throw before I saw an opening right down the middle, a near straight path to the goal line.

I was going to win this game.

I took off, my breath harsh in my own ears as I tucked the football under one arm and headed for the open pocket, the goal line in my sights. But then out the corner of my eye I spotted him.

Somehow there he was, after all the years without a word. My father had somehow managed to get himself on the sidelines. It wasn't an illusion, he was really there. I still don't know to this day how he did it, or how he got around security, but it didn't matter; the damage was done. In that moment, as he stood there with his arms across his chest staring me down, watching my every move, every single beating came rushing back. Trapped within a playing reel of my memories, I was distracted, so much so I almost stopped running. And that moment when I slowed down—did a double-take—was all it took to ruin everything.

I didn't see the defensive back come out of nowhere. He collided with me on the ten yard line, knocking the ball out. I fell hard on my side, the jarring motion rattling my teeth as I landed on the turf, watching as the ball was scooped up by the other team. There was no one there to lift me off the ground, and I was forced to walk back to the sidelines in a daze.

I tried to find the figure that had distracted me, but he was gone, and the coach grabbed my arm. I couldn't comprehend a word he was saying. I had blown it. I had single-handedly blown our chances for a playoff game.

"They wasted no time trading me," I said with a grimace, setting another bottle of beer on the table in front of me, "and you know the rest." I was spent, reliving the memories that had brought me to this present day. I looked over to see Lucia wiping tears from her eyes, a look of compassion on her face. "Shit, I didn't mean for you to cry over me."

"I'm so sorry, Jacob," she replied softly, removing the remainder of the tears from her cheeks. "I didn't know."

"There's no way you could have known, no one does. I never told anyone about what, or who, I saw that day. Or the weeks of harassment that came before that. They would've just seen it as another excuse, or that perhaps I'd really gone off the deep end and was seeing things," I interjected, wiping away her tears with my thumb. "Please don't cry, it feels good to get it off of my chest, and what's done is done. If that hadn't have happened, I wouldn't be here with you now, would I?"

"No, I guess not. Damn, I didn't mean to blub

all over you. My emotions are on overdrive."

"I get it, they're bound to be," I said. She was cute when she was flustered. "So, how do you do this every day? I mean listen to other people's problems."

She shrugged, picking at the sleeve of her blouse. "I've always had a good ear, and I guess I know when to keep my mouth closed. But mostly, it's easy; clients who come to me normally want to talk and I steer them to a resolution kinda. The want to tell their side of the story, even if it's to a complete stranger. Like you said, it's a relief, cathartic."

"You're fucking awesome," I answered, giving her a grin and pulling her close.

"Oh, shh, I'm really not. But you, you're pretty amazing. It's rare that someone comes back so strong after the hurdles you've had to overcome in your life. You need to give yourself more credit."

"I'm still a failure, though," I replied, grabbing her hand and holding it tightly. "I wasted most of my life thinking that the world owed me something in return for having a shitty father. Instead I let him get to me too many times. I should've let go of the hate and anger a long time ago." Her thumb stroked the top of my hand, and I shuddered, thinking I didn't deserve to even be sitting next to her. "But I promise you, I won't fail our child, or you, again. I swear it. I won't be like him."

"I believe you," she said, standing and tugging on my hand. "Come on."

"Wait, I need to tell you about the book you found—"

"It can wait."

Chapter Twenty Six
LUCIA

My heart was hammering in my chest as I pulled on Jacob's hand, getting him to rise off of the couch. His story tugged on my heart, clearing up a great many things about Jacob that I needed to know. Now all I saw was a little boy begging to be loved, and I was going to be that person. I was going to give him everything I had.

His hands gripped my hips and he looked at me, worry and apprehension in his eyes. "I shouldn't be here," he said quietly. "Your father will kill me."

I smiled, moving his hand from my hip to my stomach, where the life we had made together was growing. "Let me worry about that, okay?

You have already touched me in more ways than one, Jacob. There's no going back."

He looked down at his hand resting against my stomach. "I didn't mean for this to happen, to get you pregnant."

I tipped his chin up to look at me, softening my expression. "Opportunities happen when we least expect them. And yeah, it's scary, but I wouldn't change it for the world. Together we can make this work. It's more important that we look forward to our future." I swallowed. I wanted to ask him if he'd meant those words he'd said what seemed like ages ago, but what if he'd just said them in the heat of the moment? "Did you mean what you said the other day, when you said you—"

"I love you." His response was so quick it made me gasp. "One hundred percent, I meant it."

I stepped back from his touch and walked toward my bedroom. With a quick look over my shoulder I made sure he was following me. "Show me."

When I reached the bedroom, I started to strip off my clothes, my pulse pounding in my ears. But then his hand touched my bare back, I closed my eyes, my skin on fire. "Let me undress you for a change." I let my hands hang loose as he caressed my sides beneath my shirt. His movements were slow and meticulous, as if he were studying each thread of what I was wearing, teasing my skin underneath before he peeled my shirt from me.

It fell to the floor and he motioned to me to turn around. He brushed my hair to the side, letting it fall over one shoulder as his lips made contact with the tip of my shoulder, working his way up to my exposed neck, laying kisses one by one as he went. The hot air of his breath swirled and tickled my ear, and shudders like the aftershocks of an earthquake wracked my body. My bra straps fell, pushed down the slope of my upper arm by his fingers. Then his capable hands sought the clasp, but not before he ran them the length of my back, squeezing my butt for good measure.

"I don't deserve you," he breathed into my ear as he let my bra drop to the carpet. His hand wound its way to my breasts from behind, cupping them, holding them... *oh, God,* squeezing my hard nubs. "But I will have you if you will allow me to."

I exhaled. It felt so good to have his hands on me again; there was no doubt in my mind I was addicted to him. "You've always had me."

Jacob kissed my shoulder again before spinning me around, locking me tight in his arms, his eyes searching mine. I watched as his embrace loosened, and he knelt before me until his forehead was touching my stomach. I felt the tingle of my lower half as his hands slid down to cup my ass, then back around my waist to undo my trousers. He slipped those off faster, then moaned as my panty-clad pussy came into view. He pulled me closer to his mouth. When his lips touched the material, the warmth of his breath and kiss penetrated it. He increased his pressure against me; I squirmed and was rewarded with a slight squeeze.

"Stay still. Let me love you," he whispered. In one swift movement he hooked his fingers around the waistband of my panties and drew them over my hips and down around my ankles. He looked back up, his eyes directly level with my pussy. I wanted to turn away—no one had ever concentrated on me like this. But he kept me locked in place.

All of a sudden there was a cool breeze blowing onto my wetness. I fisted my hands in his hair as his tongue darted out and touched the small nub nestled between my folds, eliciting a moan deep within me. I craved his touch, wanted to feel him all over me. He was torturing me slowly with his kisses, his caresses, his tongue doing wonderful things to my oversensitive clit. When the pressure mounted again, I attempted to pull away, but he held me close until the dam burst forth and I shuddered.

Jacob wasted no time getting to his feet and getting me to lie across the bed, shedding his clothes as well before he hovered over me, spreading me wide with his large hands at my thighs. I stared at him, not wanting to miss a moment, intoxicated with the way he looked at *me*. His eyes roamed as if he wanted to see every part of my body, not wanting to miss a single bit of me, regardless of whether it was, in my opinion, not taut enough or smooth enough.

The air around us was saturated with the sweet, musky scent of sex as he burrowed deep inside me, filling me to the very core. "God, you are beautiful," he whispered, clasping our hands together as he slowly moved within me. I reached up and brushed the tips of my fingers across the side of his face, wishing I could erase the shadows from his eyes. But I would with time, if he allowed me to do so. I could be the balm he was looking for, me and this baby. Wrapping my legs around his waist, I pulled him in closer, deeper. I wanted all of him. Clenching his hands as he took me higher and higher, my pussy pulsed, pinpricks of white starlight shone bright behind my eyes, then the first waves of pleasure crashed over me like an unending barrage. It was exquisitely slow, gentle, but also deliciously hard.

I panted, my head lolling to the side as I tried to recover; I needed more. "Jacob?" I whispered, my hands going to his chest to make him slow down before he came too soon. I bit my lip, wondering what his reaction would be. I could hardly believe what I was about to ask. "Will you do that thing you did before? But this time, I want all of you inside me."

His eyes widened, shock mingling with wonderment; he understood exactly what I wanted. He nodded. "Do you have…"

With a crooked, shy smile I said, "Yes, bedside table, bottom drawer." He slid from me, the loss of him almost unbearable. But he was quick and back on the bed in no time. He knelt on the bed, cock at attention, the weight of his frame making the mattress dip slightly. He had two items in his hand, a small bottle of lube and my guilty little secret. "I found this, too, you naughty girl," he said, holding up my trusty rampant rabbit, unable to hide his grin. "My cock is so hard just thinking about you pleasuring yourself with this. But now it's my turn. Come here." I matched his pose, kneeling in front of him. Before he made me turn around, his lips sought mine, his fingers raking through my hair.

"Have you ever done this before?" he asked, and I shook my head. "I'll be gentle, don't worry. Turn around."

I did, and before I could crouch down, ready for him to be inside me again, he pulled me upright, his hands travelling up my torso to squeeze my breasts. "Not yet." He turned the rabbit on, the vibration of the little ears wiggled, then he made it disappear below. The shock of the contact on my clit made my ass judder back, but then I was wanting more. Jacob nudged the long and thick shaft of the rabbit at my entrance; it wasn't as big as him, but it still felt glorious as he started to fuck me with it. "Take over," he said, and I took hold of the vibrator. With a firm hand on my back he eased me down, my bum in the air and one hand bracing myself on the bed, while the other moved the rabbit inside my pussy.

I was already wet, drenched, but the thought of him as well as the dildo inside me sent me into overdrive.

I heard the cap of the lube bottle flip open and then as his hands spread me wide, his thumb circled over my anus, coating me with the liquid lube. I swallowed thickly as he applied more and more pressure, his thick thumb stretching me... even that little bit felt so good. Nervousness fluttered around my chest, my heart skipping a beat in anticipation and trepidation.

"Relax," he soothed as he replaced his thumb with the head of his cock. I closed my eyes, stopped thrusting the rabbit and breathed outwards as he advanced deeper. Pain mingled with a buzz of pleasure blossomed from within. "You okay?" he asked, his hands resting on my hips.

"Yes," I answered, "God, yes. More, please." He took that as a good sign and started to move slowly again, his hips swaying to and fro, giving me what I wanted.

"You feel so good," he moaned, pleasure dripped from his words, and I was so blissfully happy that I was sharing this first-time experience with him. "So tight, that's it, baby, lean back into it. Take it all."

We found a rhythm, Jacob's cock fucking me from behind, withdrawing and plunging in deep as I worked in tandem, my pussy walls wrapped around the dildo, the rabbit buzzing wildly. I was almost filled to the brim, all I needed was...

Jacob found my mouth, the tips of his fingers circling my wet lips. "Suck," he demanded, and I eagerly took the two fingers he offered me into my mouth. My tongue tasted the remnants of my own juices on his skin and I started to suck as Jacob took a handful of tit and squeezed, pinching so hard I saw stars.

My senses were overloading as he continued to fuck my ass. In equal measure my chest and pussy felt they were going to explode. I moaned around his digits, panting, forcing air through my nose… God, I didn't want this feeling to stop. It was too much and yet at the same time not enough.

I let go of the vibrator, and he claimed my hips, using them as leverage as he greedily thrust into me again and again. Harder with each stroke.

"Fuck, yes!" I screamed, my orgasm detonating as my tits bounced freely.

Jacob tensed and my toes curled. He swelled within me, his cock feeling like it was doubling in size. I turned slightly, looked over my shoulder, and saw the muscles in his jaw as they became taut. Our eyes met and a second later he roared, his seed spurting and filling my ass before he collapsed on top of me, his breathing harsh in my ear.

* * *

We lay like that for I don't know how long, his cock still inside me, his hand idly nestled between my legs, cupping my sex, rubbing me gently till I came again. "I can't stop touching you," he said, once I was spent.

We coiled around each other, and I ran my hands over his broad, muscular shoulders, tracing my fingers down his spine. His head rested upon my breast, a pillow under his sweating brow.

As if demonstrating his words were true, his tongue reached out and licked at my softening nipple, causing it to crease up and harden once more. He leaned his head up to look at me, a roguish smile on his face. "Hey, beautiful."

"Hey, yourself," I said, falling for him harder than I ever thought possible. "I must confess, that was the best therapy session I've ever had."

He let out a laugh. "I hope I'm the only one that gets this kind of VIP treatment," he said with a wink before sliding off of me.

"You're the first… and only."

That made him grin again. I watched as he stood and stretched, admiring his naked body. Every part of him was perfect, tight and hard; the perks of dating an athlete, I thought, as I continued to ogle the eye candy before me. I rose up on my elbows, not even thinking about covering myself, I was that comfortable around him, and after what we'd just done, I had better be. The green glow from clock in the darkening room told me it was getting late, and my stomach growled. "Hey, are you hungry?"

Jacob gathered up his clothes and started replacing them hastily one by one, suddenly nervous. "I would stay, but I've got to get out of here before your dad finds me, Lucia."

I sighed and climbed off the bed, striding to the closet and pulling down a thin dressing gown. I slid it over my naked body but left the ties undone. "I think him finding you here is the least of our problems, Jacob. Besides, it doesn't matter anymore. He will have to get over it." A thought hit me and I turned back to him, biting my lip. I'd been so swept up in our combined emotions that we hadn't really discussed what was going to happen. "You do want to continue this, right?" If he said no, I was going to die. Based on his earlier remarks, I knew he was going to be there for our child, but was it a package deal, or was I just going to be his baby's mama?

Jacob dropped his shirt over his head before looking at me, a searing glance that caused my knees to weaken slightly. "Like you even need to ask that question. Hell, yes, I want you and the baby both." His hands sought my waist, brushing past the silk of the dressing gown. "We are going to continue—I would fuck you, make love to you, all damn day and night if I could, but I'd rather your dad found out while we had our clothes on, and not here in the throes of passion."

"O-oh," I said, thinking that he was probably right about that.

Jacob tenderly pushed a stray hair out of my face. "Babe, I'm going to take care of you.

I'm not going to let you go. We'll figure how all this will work with me being a player on your father's team and you employed there, too. We'll find a way. I'll take care of you if you want to quit, if that makes things easier, but something tells me that you'd rather continue to work, and I am cool with that, as well. You are good at what you do, and you have worked extremely hard to get where you are today."

My eyes teared up, and he kissed me softly. "Don't cry."

"Well, you better get used to it if you say things like that," I replied. "I hear pregnant women cry all the time."

"Well, I will have to make sure we buy a load of tissues then." He grinned, gathering me up in his arms. I laid my head on his shoulder, breathing in the heady scent of him.

"I have something to tell you."

"It's not twins, is it?"

I laughed; I hadn't even considered that possibility. "Erm, no, at least I don't think so. That would be insane… One baby is more than enough, I think. Don't you?"

He nodded, his hands running up and down my back. "What were you going to tell me then?"

"Oh, right, yes. I've already decided I'm going to leave the team. Strike out on my own, well, with a partner, my friend Cara." I told him our plan, and he seemed genuinely excited for me.

"Ah, such a shame though, I won't be able to see you at the stadium any time I want, and that desk of yours... I haven't had the chance to bend you over it."

I laughed and swatted at him. "There will be plenty opportunity to do that in my new office."

Jacob pulled back and kissed me again. "So what's our next step?"

"With what?" I asked, a thousand thoughts running through my mind. I was going to have to go public with this relationship eventually, including the baby, but I preferred to do it in my own time. First, though, I was going to have to break the news to my father, which was scary in itself. The baby was probably going to make things easier with getting him to accept our relationship, and I just hoped that Jacob wasn't going to take the brunt of the blame for all of this. I had been a very willing participant.

"With supper," he said, causing me to relax slightly, "I'm starving. Do we want to go out or order in at my place?"

I thought of the nice swimming pool in his

backyard and smiled. "Yours, of course. Just let me grab a few things."

"You won't need much. You're going to be butt-naked if I have my way."

* * *

I nervously sat down at my father's dining room table, giving both him and Merry a small smile. Tonight was the night I was going to tell them the wonderful news. I hoped I wouldn't be disowned by the end of the night. Jacob had offered to join me, to be by my side as I told them, but I knew this was something I had to do on my own, and I had to do it sooner rather than later—I couldn't wait any more. Besides, things were likely to get heated if Jacob turned up out of the blue. Anyway he was, after all, meant to be working tonight.

"So," Merry started out, tucking her napkin in her lap. "I have to say, Lucia, your father and I were a bit surprised that you felt the need to request our presence at dinner."

"I just wanted to make sure you both were here and I know it's a busy night," I said, drawing in a breath, "but I have something important to discuss with both of you."

"We might have to cut it short, I have a game to watch. But if it's about your job, I've already heard that bit," my father replied, his eyes darkening.

"How dare the team think they can go on strike and not attend your therapy sessions? They're in breach of contract. I'll have their balls."

"Oh, please don't do that," I said hastily as the first course was served. "I-I'm leaving the team, Daddy."

"You're what?" he asked, his expression one of surprise. "Leaving? But why? I thought this was your dream?"

"It's my dream to help people," I replied, fiddling with my napkin. "And as much as I like being around the stadium, it's obvious to me at least that I am a distraction, something that is being forced on them rather than the guys or the staff reaching out to me. That was not my intention."

My father's expression grew darker, and he templed his fingers together over his soup. "Did someone say something to you, Lucia?"

"No," I lied, not wanting to throw anyone under the bus. Looking back, I realized that all Greg's snide remarks were not because he hated me. He wanted his guys to focus on their jobs regardless of the help I could provide, and I was willing to step away from the distraction. After all, I had helped some of them, including Jacob. Just the thought of him brought a tremor through my body. I was already missing his handsome face after two days of being solely in his company. If Merry or my father had noted my absence from the guest house, neither of them had said so. Instead I had enjoyed two long days at Jacob's home, where he'd told me all the ins and outs of the little black book I'd found. Some of what he'd told me was hard to hear but my heart had already forgiven him, and we spent the remaining time contemplating our future together.

He'd been absent for some of the weekend, getting ready for the Monday night game, but we'd managed to fit in enough time with each other. He was traveling to the away game in Massachusetts, and though he had all but begged me to join him, to delay the inevitable, I'd declined, knowing that I wanted to talk to my father first.

"No one has said anything to me, Daddy. This is my decision. And I have decided to go into private practice with Cara. You remember Cara?"

"Your friend from university?" he asked evenly, taking in every word I was saying with more calm than I'd given him credit for. "She's in Jupiter?"

"Starting her own practice," I replied proudly. He knew Cara had worked hard to be where she was today too, and I couldn't wait to join her on this journey. "I start in a few days."

My father looked at me, concern in his eyes. "Are you sure about this, Lucia?"

I looked at him and smiled. "I've never been more sure in my life. This is what I need to do. My next step. It will be good, I promise. I'm so grateful to you for giving me my first real shot, but it's time to move on. Make my own way, like you did."

After a beat, digesting my words, he nodded. "I'm going to miss having you around."

"You won't be getting rid of me. I'll still be there on the sidelines with you."

"I am so proud of you," Merry interjected, giving me a smile. "Who knows? Maybe you will become the therapist to the league!"

"I'm proud of you too, baby girl," my father said, using the nickname he called me when I was younger. "Whatever makes you happy makes us happy. You have my full support in everything you do."

"Everything?" I questioned, a tiny laugh bubbled to the surface, giving away more.

"Yes…" he said with a frown. "Why do you say it like that?"

"Because there's more," I rushed out. Time to rip the band-aid off. "I'm pregnant."

Merry's smile dimmed a little and her eyes widened. "Pregnant?"

I nodded, stealing a look at my father. His spoon was still suspended in the air, a look of utter shock and surprise on his face. "A few weeks. You are going to be grandparents."

My father set his spoon down in his bowl with a clatter. I bit my tongue, waiting for his full reaction. It was either going to go smoothly, or it was about to get very, very loud.

"How on earth!? But you haven't been dating? I don't understand. How did this happen?" He shook his head, trying to gather his thoughts, his face turning a deepening shade of red. "Who's the father? Do I know him?"

I nodded again, knowing that this was the hardest part of the entire conversation. "It's Jacob Maddox. But before you say anything—"

"A player? You were fraternizing with the players?" he shot back. His fist slammed on the table and caused the other plates to rattle in response.

"No, Daddy. Not players—just the one." But either he didn't hear me, or he didn't want to.

"How many times have I warned you about them, Lucia? Oh God, this is really going to throw a spanner in the campaign. I can't believe you did this, not now, not while I'm running for mayor. What will people think?"

"It just sort of happened, and I don't care what people think!" I responded, hearing the shame in his voice. It tore me nearly in half to think I had disappointed him. "It was mutual, Daddy. I'm in love with him, and he's in love with me."

"Love! Bah! Jacob fucking Maddox," he repeated, a thunderous look on his face. "I knew it. He has been sniffing around you for weeks! Don't you think I haven't noticed? I know everything that goes on in my team!"

"And I have been allowing him to do just that," I said hotly, hating the way this was going. It was like talking to a brick wall. He'd already decided to hate Jacob and obviously believed he had a full say in who I would end up with; if he didn't approve, then it was a no-go. I stood up, and my forgotten napkin fluttered to the floor.

"I'm an adult, in case you haven't noticed. A grown woman, and I can make decisions on who I date and what I do. I don't need your approval or polls to tell me what I should or shouldn't do. And I choose to tell you things about my life because I want to share them with you, but that doesn't mean I need your permission to do them." I was on the verge of tears and ready to leave.

"And just so you know, we are both extremely excited about this baby. We are going to be a family no matter what happens. No matter what you say or do. If you decide to fire Jacob based on something that has nothing to do with his job, then—"

"Lucia, sweetie, sit down," Merry interrupted. "You should know better. Your father is not going to anything of the sort, are you, David?"

He cleared his throat. I think he was a little taken aback at how fiercely I'd stuck to my guns. I'd never spoken to either of them like that before, never had the need to before now—but I just hoped it proved how much Jacob and the baby meant to me.

"No. I won't fire him. But he's crossed a line, Lucia—"

"Hush, David! This is a happy occasion. Your only daughter has just told you she's with child. Gosh, a baby, so exciting!" Merry continued, a knowing smile returning on her face. "I'm going to be a grandma. Oh lord, do I have to be called grandma? Can it be like Nana Merry or something, well, not so old?"

"You can call yourself whatever you like," I laughed, glad that I had her on my side. Not that I doubted she would be. I looked back at my father and reached out, touching his arm. "Jacob is a good man, Daddy. He's had his issues, but he's working through them. You'll see when you get to know him better. He's *right* for me."

After a few tense moments, my father laid his hand over mine, the warmth of his touch thawing the ice that stood between us. "I see that now. I don't think I've seen you happier than now. Congratulations, baby girl. I know you'll be a wonderful mother, and Merry and I will support you and Jacob however we can."

Tears sprang to my eyes as I realized he'd given us his blessing. "Thank you. Will you at least try to be nice to Jacob?" I asked softly.

My father grunted and turned back to his soup as Merry gave me a wink. She leaned over and whispered in my ear, "So when do I get to meet the hunk?"

All was going to be okay. Well, at least Jacob wasn't going before the firing squad any time soon.

* * *

After dinner I figured it was time to tell Cara what was going on. I got her to meet me at our favorite bar, finding her already sitting there with two drinks on the table when I arrived.

"Hey, you sounded stressed, so I ordered you a drink," she responded as I took a seat on the stool. "Your favorite."

I eyed the fruity concoction that I so enjoyed drinking and sighed, knowing that for at least eight months or so it would be off the menu. "I can't drink it."

"Of course you can!" she said, pushing it toward me with a grin. "Geez, we can get a taxi if we're going to get sloshed tonight."

"No," I said, giving her a look. "I can't drink it at all."

Cara's grin faded as she looked at me closely, her expression going to complete surprise in an instant. "Oh my God, you're knocked up!"

"Um, yeah, I am," I said, a smile playing on my lips. Cara always had a way with words.

"Wow," Cara replied, looking down at my stomach. "I can't believe it. This is all so out of the blue!"

"Yeah, tell me about it," I admitted, pushing the drink back her way. She drained hers before reaching for mine. "I'm going to be an auntie. That kid is going to be spoiled rotten. Shit, have you told your father? He's going to freak."

I nodded and told her about the dinner with my parents, then signaled the waitress and asked for a ginger ale. If the nausea didn't go away soon, it was going to be a miserable eight months.

"So," she continued, her eyes bright with curiosity. "Will there be some Jacob Maddox baby-daddy drama on the way?"

"There's no drama," I replied with a roll of my eyes, biting my lip to stop the grin that was trying desperately to form. "Everything is good, *really* good. Like beyond good, amazing even."

"Wait," Cara suddenly said, arching a brow. "You love him, don't you?"

I felt my breath leave my chest as I thought about what Jacob meant to me. This was way beyond the little life we had created together. What I felt for him ran very deep, deeper than any feeling I had ever experienced. I missed him when we weren't together. I craved him. "Yes," I finally said, drawing in a breath. "I love him."

"Oh, snap," Cara replied, her eyes widening. "This is serious? Like settling down serious. Has he asked you to, you know?"

"Very serious," I sighed, taking a sip of my ginger ale. I was truly sunk in love, but could it be such a bad thing to be in love with a wonderful man such as Jacob? We'd had our bumps, but we were smoothing them out. What couple didn't have a few glitches when starting out?

"But, no, he hasn't asked me to marry him. We haven't even talked about it… I think it might be too soon for that, you know?"

"Do you want him to ask you?"

"I'm not sure. I mean, we can be together and have a baby without the whole marriage part, right?"

"Yeah, of course, it's the twenty-first century, anything goes," she said with a laugh. "Well you must have talked about the baby, though." Cara continued. "Is he fully on board? Or is this going to turn into *Two Women and a Baby*?"

"Oh no," I said, laughing. "He's definitely on board. I think this is it, Cara. I think I've found my happily ever after."

"Well, it's about time," she exclaimed, draining her drink. "At least I have something to spend my money on now. Can I put in a vote for a girl?"

I laughed again, the rest of my worry melting away. This was going to work. I had full support of my parents, Cara, and Jacob. That was all that mattered.

It was almost too good to be true.

Chapter Twenty Seven
JACOB

"**A**re you sure you want to do this, son?"

I looked down at the paperwork I'd finished filling out, a ball of red hot emotion settling in my chest. After the bombshell Lucia had dropped on me a few days ago, coupled with the fact that I never wanted to have to worry about her safety ever again, I'd gone to the local courthouse to file a restraining order against my own father. I couldn't take the risk of him popping up whenever he felt like it, getting in my face again or harassing the mother of my child. I didn't want him in my life any longer and was willing to take drastic measures in order for that not to happen.

I'd also found out from Coach that they'd banned my father from all games and had also gone whole hog and gotten a restraining order on him, too. He was unable to set foot within a thousand feet of any building considered part of the team's facility. Somehow, I managed to come out smelling like roses—the PR team spun the incident to make me look like a hero. I didn't take much pleasure in that story, though. I knew I had lost my temper, knew I'd been wrong, but I wasn't about to tell the police it was my fault and get my father off the hook for all the abuse he'd shelled out to me or my mother over the years.

The officers who later questioned me asked if I wanted to press charges, and though Lucia urged me to do so, I didn't want it dragging on. It would only draw more attention, there'd be a media circus for weeks to come, and I still needed to keep my head clear for work.

Signing my name on the line, I pushed the paperwork toward the clerk. "I'm sure. Does it go into effect immediately?"

"It'll go to the judge first, then there will be a hearing," the clerk replied, standing. "I'll have it there before lunch, Mr. Maddox, and you'll hear in the next few days about the hearing."

"Okay, good. Thanks for your help."

"No problem. Thank you for the autograph; my son is going to go nuts over it!"

I shook his hand and walked out of the court house, surprised to find Lucia's father standing beside a large SUV. "Get in," he said, his eyes hidden behind a pair of dark glasses. "We need to talk."

I swallowed hard and climbed in, hoping that this wasn't going to be the last ride I ever took as a Jupiter Suns quarterback. The SUV pulled away from the curb, destination unknown, and I didn't care to ask. We rode in silence for a while as I fidgeted with the cuff of my sleeve, wondering how this was going to end.

"You disobeyed me, and now she's pregnant," he finally said, breaking the silence. "Care to tell me how that happened when I warned you to stay away from her?"

"Sir, with all due respect, I don't think you want to know how it happened, and I can assure you, it was not planned. But it doesn't matter how it happened; we love each other."

"Lucia said that as well," he said gruffly. "What do you want from my family, Mr. Maddox?"

Caught off guard, I looked at him to find the man who signed my paychecks staring at me intently, his glasses now nowhere to be seen. "What?"

"If it's money, I can provide it—there'd be

conditions, of course," he continued on, clearing his throat. "You already have the starting position on the team. I can extend that for as long as I need to, provided you stay away from her."

"That's not going to happen."

I thought about the away game the other night and how for the first time in a long while, I was able to concentrate effectively on the game, knowing that I had Lucia waiting at home. I stuck to the plays, and in the end we were able to pull out a win. It had been the best damn game I'd had in years. "I'm not trying to scam you or your daughter," I said slowly. "I don't want anything from you, sir."

Surprise filtered through his expression, and I grinned. "I have everything I need: a baby on the way and a fine woman who loves me for me, and a well-paying job—that's if I still have one, of course. What else could I want?"

"Do you truly love my daughter?" he asked briskly as the SUV slowed down in front of the stadium. I started then, my heart hammering in my chest. Love was too short a word for what I felt for her. I respected her for everything she had been through and for the hell I had put her through, yet she kept on wanting to be with me. Any man was damn lucky to have a woman like her by his side.

"You should already know the answer to that, Mr. Cortes. But just in case you're unclear, I love her more than the game we call football," I finally said, feeling something in my chest break free.

"Good answer," he replied, slapping me on the back, a smile breaking free. *Fuck,* it had all been a test, and it seemed like I'd passed. "Welcome to the family, son. Now get the hell out of my car and win me some games. You're gonna have a mouth to feed soon."

I grinned and exited as quickly as I could, before he could change his mind. I called a cab and went back to the courthouse to get my car, then drove to Lucia's new place of business to pick her up and to tell her what had just happened. She'd be happy to know we hadn't ripped each other's throats out and could be civil. I had other things to tell her, as well, things that were on my chest that I desperately needed to share with her.

She was lugging a box up the steps of the townhouse that was her and Cara's new office space, and I leaped out of the car to stop her. "I told you, you shouldn't be carrying things."

I took the box from her and kissed her hello. "Don't be silly, it's good exercise. Besides I'm not even showing yet."

"Yeah, I suppose. I just want you to be careful."

She nodded. "I will."

"So how did everything go this morning?"

"It was… interesting," I said. "Did you already finish moving? I said I'd help."

"It's okay, I didn't have much," she said as I grabbed her hand, and together we walked inside. "I got everything moved in today. But there are some shelves you can put up if you're willing."

"Anything for you," I replied, giving her a squeeze. I was going to miss having her right down the hall. "You ready to go?" She nodded and locked up again.

Today was a very important day. Today was going to be the first time we'd hear our child's heartbeat. We were both nervous and fidgety when we got to the clinic—but neither of us could stop smiling. I watched as Lucia signed herself in, and then we settled onto a bench together, our hands still clasped. "So," I said casually, stretching my legs out in front of me, "I got a visit from your father today."

"What?" she asked, turning toward me. "Oh dear God, what did he do?"

"Nothing," I chuckled, releasing her hand to stretch my arm along the back of the bench. "Well, he had me going for a bit.

He asked me a few questions and then dropped me off at the stadium, still in one piece."

"What kind of questions? He asked you how it happened, didn't he?"

"No, of course not," I replied, hoping the little white lie would take away her look of mortification, then gave her a serious look. "He did make me think, though, and I have something I want to ask you."

"Okay," she said as my fingers stroked the back of her neck. I sucked in a breath, suddenly feeling lightheaded. What if she didn't agree? What if I wasn't ready? The nerves were worse than any major game I had ever played in. "He asked me if I loved you, Lucia, and you already know I do, don't you?"

"Yes," she said, drawing out the word slowly. "I love you, too."

"I told him yes, of course," I finally said. "But my conversation with your father made me realize I can't live without you. Literally. I feel like part of me is missing when you're not with me."

"Oh, Jacob," she breathed, her eyes misting with those ever-present tears. I was getting used to them, especially after the other night where we had watched some sappy movie in my bed and she had cried her way through it. A box of tissues was a handy thing to have in practically every room of my house now.

"So, I want you to move in with me. Right now, today, as soon as possible, Lucia. I mean you liked the house, didn't you? But if you don't, I can buy another one, anywhere you like, anything you want. We can start working on the nursery. You pick any room in whichever house you choose, but maybe not our bedroom—"

She placed a finger over my lips, silencing me. "Shh, you're cute when you ramble, you know?"

"Is that a yes?"

"Of course it is, you love-sick fool. I don't want to be away from you, either. And I like how you say it's ours," she responded, moving her fingers to my face. "I'm so happy, Jacob."

"Me too," I found myself saying, a grin on my face. Hell, I was more than happy, I was ecstatic.

"Lucia Cortes?"

I looked up and found a nurse smiling down at us. "Come on, babe, it's time to meet our little lovebug."

Chapter Twenty Eight
LUCIA

I sat back on my heels and looked around the office, a smile on my face. The space was really shaping up to be something wonderful. Most of my diplomas were already hanging on the wall adjacent to the beautiful windows that gave me a partial view of the beach and the water beyond. A potted plant stood in one corner, a gift of sorts from my father to congratulate me on my new practice. And though I could still feel his worry and concern about my new move and my new man, he was coming around, warming up to seeing Jacob and me as a couple. I was glad he had reached out to Jacob on his own, and they had both survived the meeting unscathed.

"Lucia?"

I looked up to see Cara in the doorway, looking every inch the therapist I knew her to be. "There's someone to see you."

I pushed off the floor and straightened my pencil skirt, giving her a nod. "Okay, show them in." I didn't have anyone scheduled yet, but a walk-in this early must be a good sign, I thought.

She grinned and pushed away from the door as I nervously twisted my hands together, wondering who it could be. I didn't have to wait long.

"Greg?"

The head coach of the Jupiter Suns walked into my office—the last person I ever imagined. He had his ever-present baseball cap with him, but instead of being on his head to cover his bald spot, it was in his hands, and he twisted the material to and fro. "Lucia. Is this a bad time?"

"N-no of course not," I responded, surprised that he was here. "Come in, have a seat."

He gave me a small smile as he seated himself on the couch while I closed the door, curiosity drumming in my veins. I walked to the chair opposite and sat down on the edge. "Can I get you something, water or juice, perhaps?"

"No, I'm good," he said, clearing his throat. "I'm just going to come straight out with it.

I've come to apologize. I didn't give you a fair shake from day one, even though I knew you were only trying to help out. Lucia, I've known you for years, and you have a good heart. But all this, the head-shrinking stuff, it never sat well with me."

There was a story behind that explanation, but I didn't press. Now wasn't the time.

"I-I don't know what to say," I said slowly. I was still trying to process that Coach Hanshield was in my office apologizing to *me*. Talk about an interesting turn of events, indeed.

"Say you will forgive me?" Greg asked, his eyes full of remorse. "And no, before you ask, your father didn't ask me to do this. This is all me. After the way you handled Maddox, I have to say you know what you are doing. I thought he was going to kill that man."

"You and me both," I admitted, my thoughts going back to the confrontation with Jacob's father. The good thing was that both my father and Jacob had put out restraining orders on him so I didn't have to worry about him coming around anymore. I think he got the message, crystal clear, that last time. I hoped to never see him again, or I was going to kill him myself. Jacob didn't need him popping up out of the blue all the time. Though, I had to give Jacob more credit than I was doing, he seemed to have let go all of the anger he'd been storing up against his father, and if Marshall ever did violate the restraining order, I had a feeling Jacob would just let the event wash over him like water off a duck's back.

"I don't know how you did it, but he's a changed man. A completely different player. He's more focused than ever before. I'd even hasten to say he's better than he ever was in his college football glory days. I've seen and compared the tapes—he's on fire."

"I can't take all the credit, Greg. We're a team. You and your coaches built him up, gave him the confidence he needed. It's just a shame Danny had to get hurt for Jacob to shine. How is he, by the way? I've been thinking about him."

"Not so good. He's talking about retirement even though I know he's far from done. Actually, I wanted to ask you a favor."

"Anything."

"I'm going to send Danny to you, if that's okay? I've talked to him, and he's game if you are."

"It'd be my pleasure. Tell him to call, and I'll get him an appointment straight away. We'll get him through this rough patch together." He nodded, and I sensed he wasn't done. "Is there anything else on your mind, Greg?"

So," Greg continued, looking a bit nervous now. "I was wondering if you, well, if you can fit me into your schedule, too."

"Really?" I asked, surprised for the second time in a matter of minutes. "Why is that?"

"To be brutally honest, I'm struggling. Always on the road, the games, the pressure of it all… it's starting to get to me," he said softly, suddenly looking a great deal older. "My wife, she complains that I am testy when I am at home; I can't switch off. I think I just need to talk it out and would like to bring her in to talk, as well, when the time's right."

I smiled at him then and pulled out a fresh notebook. "I think that would be a great idea. I have some free time now, if you want to strike while the iron is hot."

He swallowed. He and I both knew he was taking a big step, and he nodded again.

"Okay then," I said with a reassuring smile. "Tell me, what's been going on?"

* * *

"Here's your next appointment. I will schedule them weekly unless you tell me otherwise."

The coach looked up at me and squeezed my hand lightly. "Thank you for listening, Lucia. There's no one else I would trust."

"Not a problem." I smiled as I showed him to the door. When I opened it, Jacob was standing there, causing my heart to flutter in my chest wildly. His look of surprise was priceless, and he opened his mouth to speak before I gave him a firm shake of my head, pushing past him to usher the coach out. When he was gone, I turned around, finding him grinning at me. "Really? Coach?"

"Client-therapist confidentiality," I immediately said, standing on my toes to kiss him. "I can't say anything else."

"Well that, I guess, is a good thing," Jacob replied, sneaking another kiss in. "I've got a surprise for you, as well."

"You do?" I asked as we walked into my office. He nodded and shut the door, leaning against it. I found my breath increasing as I took in his handsome features, wondering if maybe we could be quiet enough to do it right here. The thought crossed my mind, and I grinned, causing Jacob to grin as well. "What are you thinking?" he asked softly.

"I'll tell you later," I said, leaning suggestively against the desk. "What's your news?"

"Well, I hope you don't take this the wrong way, but as you know, I have some issues," he responded with a laugh. "So, I decided to seek out another therapist. I start next week. Don't worry, it's a guy! I made sure. I just don't think we'd get much done if I continued with our unofficial sessions."

"Oh my God, that is great! And, no, I get it," I exclaimed, happy that he acknowledged that he needed to see someone professionally. "It'll be good for you. But who did you go to? I could've given you a recommendation."

"I know. I just wanted to do this on my own. I found a great guy, though. Maybe you've heard of him—Dr. Harris?"

I raised my eyebrow; I knew the name very well. "Oh, I see," I said teasingly, "you chose my direct competition over me."

He laughed and pulled me into his arms. "I couldn't have done it without you, of course," Jacob said. "I think you are turning the bad boy into something respectable."

"Well I hope the bad boy is not all gone... I think I might need him for something."

He reached out and gripped my hips with his hands, the heat in his eyes unmistakable. "Oh really? And what's that exactly?"

Boldly, I reached down and cupped him, feeling the hardness against the palm of my hand. "Well, we haven't christened my new office yet."

His eyes dilated as his hands slid up my sides. "God, you are so sexy when you talk like that."

"I can hear you! You better not be naked 'cause I'm coming in!"

Surprised, we jumped apart as the door opened and Cara stormed in, her eyes full of laughter. "Geez, guys, get a room, will you?"

"We have a room," I said laughing. I darted in front of Jacob in attempts to hide his erection from view, but she gave me a knowing look. "Jacob, this is Cara. Cara, this is Jacob."

"Finally we meet! I've heard a lot about you," Cara said, sticking out her hand. "And if you are half the man Lucia brags about, then you're okay in my *playbook*."

I groaned and gave her a wicked stare.

"Thanks, I think," Jacob replied hesitantly, shaking her hand. "I've heard a lot about you, as well."

Cara released his hand and looked at me, a grin on her face. "Were you really about to do the dirty in the office? I mean we haven't even been here a week! But carry on, I won't stop you. So damn lucky."

My face turned red as Jacob choked on his laughter, smothering it with a cough. "Cara."

"What?" she asked. "Now you're embarrassed? At least someone's getting some!" She giggled and backed away to the door. "I'll leave you to it. Just wait till I'm out of earshot, okay?"

I shook my head and she turned to leave. "Nice to meet you, Jacob. You break her heart, I break your pretty-boy face. Got it?" Cara disappeared, and I burst into laughter. She was a hard-ass, but I loved her.

"Is she always like that? I don't know who I'm more scared of, her or your father," Jacob said, a grin on his face. "There are huge football players that would be terrified of crossing her, and I'm one of them."

"I highly don't recommend it," I giggled, clasping his hand in mine. "Come on, I'm hungry. We can christen the office later." I pulled Jacob toward the door but was tugged back against him, his hands wrapping around me. "You know I am not going to let you down, right?"

I spun around in his arms, seeing the serious look on his face. "Are you seriously concerned about Cara? She's all talk, I swear."

His grin was adorable. "No, I'm not worried about Cara. I just don't want to disappoint you, Lucia. I-I feel like I'm walking in a dream, having you and our little lovebug in my life. I don't want to wake up."

"Aww," I said softly, reaching up to touch his face. "Don't let anyone tell you that you aren't completely and utterly sweet." Brushing my lips over his, I looked deep into his eyes. "Babe, I have nothing but faith in you. I love you. That's all that matters."

"And I love you," he said, his gaze softening. "Come on, let's feed the both of you."

Chapter Twenty Nine
JACOB

I put my bag in my locker and pulled out the small picture from my back pocket, positioning it just inside the small shelf. My chest ached as I looked at it. Never in my wildest dreams would I have imagined posting a pic of an ultrasound in my locker and feeling fucking awesome about it, but I couldn't be prouder. I had helped create the little bug in the picture, and I was determined going to be the best damn father to him or her.

"Dude! What the hell is happening in your life?"

Grinning, I turned to Terrence, seeing the look of amusement and shock as he looked up at the picture. "I'm gonna be a daddy."

"That's, um, that's great," he said slowly, eyeing me. "Right?"

"Fuck, yeah!" I replied, that warm feeling wrapping around my body once more. I wasn't going to regret this part of my life. Every day with Lucia made me realize how petty my life had gotten, and how close I had been to throwing away something that most athletes dream about. I'd been lucky to have someone who cared that I was screwing up and helped me get back on the right track.

"With Lucia?" Terrence asked, pulling me out of my thoughts. I nodded and he slapped me on the back, a grin on his face. "Dude! I can't believe you were actually able to reel her in and get her knocked up!"

"Well, I have to thank you for that, I guess," I responded, pulling my pads over my shoulders and adjusting them. "After all, you were the one with that stupid book."

Terrence looked at me, then busted out laughing, holding his gut with his forearm. "The playbook? It was a complete fake. We do it to all the new guys, and most of them find out real quick that the names in there are not even real. Even the phone numbers are pure fabrication."

Puzzled, I crossed my arms over my chest. "You mean it's all fake? But Lucia's name was in there."

Terrence had the grace to look slightly embarrassed, the laughter dying down.

"Yeah, well, you were the only one to find that out. Not that the things written in there were true, but we were just testing the new guys to see if any would bite. You were the first one."

I thought about how I had seen her as a challenge at first, a way to prove myself to everyone else. Instead she helped me see that I didn't need anyone else's approval but my own. "You know what?" I finally said, slapping Terrence on the back this time. "I think you did me a favor."

"You aren't pissed?" he asked, surprised. I shook my head and pointed to the ultrasound, my reason for living now. "How could I be pissed when I have that to look forward to?"

Terrence shook his head in return, a genuine smile on his face now. "Yeah, I guess you're right. I guess you have me to thank for your happy little life now."

"True. You might want to make it up to Lucia somehow, though."

"Shit, she knows?"

"Of course."

"Mmm, consider it done. We'll do something special."

I laughed and threw my towel at him. "Come on. Let's go kick some second-string ass."

"Hey, do you still have the book?" he asked as we walked toward the locker room exit, filing out for another day of hard practicing.

"I think it ended up on the owner's desk," I said casually. Terrence almost tripped over his own feet, his eyes widening in horror. "Are you serious?" he whispered. "Please, God, don't tell me you are serious."

I grinned then, walking ahead of him. "I can't confirm or deny that statement. Maybe you should ask Lucia what she did with it." Terrence swore under his breath, and I broke out into a whistle as I hit the field.

Chapter Thirty
LUCIA

I fought the urge to bite my nails as I watched Greg call a time-out. Jacob ran to the sideline to coordinate with him. It was the final game of the regular season, the one that decided whether or not we went to the playoffs. Currently, the team was tied with another in the division, and a win tonight would push us over the top. With a minute left, there were only six points between us and the playoffs. One touchdown was all we needed.

The referee blew the whistle, and I pressed my hand over my belly, feeling the small flutter of movement in response. She was a flurry of activity tonight, excited like I was for her daddy.

When we found out that the baby was a girl, Jacob burst into tears. I had thought he would've been disappointed that it wasn't a boy, but I was way wrong.

"Wow," he said, wiping his face with his hand. "A girl. I can't believe it."

"Are you disappointed?" I asked hesitantly, knowing that most men wanted a boy, a little miniature copy of themselves to play ball with. Jacob shook his head, his eyes glimmering with tears. "She's never gonna want for anything, Lucia. I will protect her with my very life. But she's not dating till she's at least thirty!"

It had been the sweetest thing I'd ever heard, and I promptly burst into tears with him, which was something I did on a pretty frequent basis.

But now, now the focus was on Jacob and the chance to fulfill one of his lifelong dreams—go to the playoffs and win the Super Bowl. I was nervous for him, but not as nervous as my father, who was currently wearing down the grass on the sideline, walking briskly with his hands clasped behind his back. This was going to be the pivotal moment to prove that he hadn't made a bad investment. At his urging, Jacob and I had done a joint interview with the newspaper to try to smooth over the bad publicity that Jacob's father had brought forth. Jacob had really opened up and talked about his childhood, though he left some of the more disturbing details out it. Then he turned to his future with the team.

We also went public with our relationship and the pregnancy, knowing full well I wouldn't be able to hide it much longer. Overall, the article had been well received, and I felt like Jacob was understood and accepted here in Jupiter. My dad's campaign was in full swing, as well, which was another reason we wanted to air our 'dirty laundry', but right now the polls seemed favorable to him—the little scandal hadn't caused too much of a fuss.

But, if Jacob didn't get the win tonight, I feared all his hard work would be overshadowed by one loss. He'd be back in the limelight again, the backlash would be fierce, old dirt would be dug up again and again.

Up until now we'd been living almost in a dream state. I thoroughly enjoyed waking up next to him in the morning, loved watching him as he caressed my growing stomach tenderly before we got ready for our busy day ahead. And then coming home from work to find him there, waiting to hear about my day and vice versa. It was everything I never knew I'd lacked until now and with the unlikeliest of characters making me deliriously happy. I couldn't imagine anyone else.

We would weather the outcome of this game together as best we could, whatever happened, but I still kept my fingers crossed just in case.

The offense broke the huddle, and Jacob trotted to his position behind the center, his eyes shifting left then right as he called out a series of plays. The crowd seemed to come to a dull roar as the ball was snapped. I held my breath as Jacob looked for an open receiver, his feet dancing around the turf to keep himself out of harm's way. Then he let go of the ball, the entire stadium watching as it sailed thirty yards to the open receiver near the end zone. The ball soared directly into his open arms—a direct hit—and he took it over the line.

I stood there, mesmerized, as the crowd went wild and Jacob thrust his arms into the air, the referee signaling touchdown just as the time clock wound its way to zero. He had done it! We were going to the playoffs! The sideline erupted, and I clapped excitedly, following my father as he rushed out onto the field and high-fived the players as they came back to the bench.

Jacob jogged to the end zone, a shocked look on his face as he pulled off his helmet and hugged his wide receiver, number 27—Terrence Gold—lifting him high in the air. They'd worked so well together in practice that Greg had had no choice but to bump Terrence up to first string.

And now that decision was definitely paying off.

"You did it!" I exclaimed as I waddled towards him. It was totally unorthodox for me to be on the field, but I dared anyone to stop me. He put Terrence down and ran to meet me, gently hugging me as we came together. "I did it."

"Playoffs, baby!" I laughed as he kissed me soundly on the lips.

"Yeah," he said with a grin, wiping the sweat off his face then stripping off the glove from his throwing hand. "I can't believe it. Oh my God, we are going to the fucking playoffs. This is, fuck, I don't know what to say."

"I knew you could do it," I grinned, putting my hands on either side of his face and kissing his lips, tasting the tangy saltiness on them from the four rough quarters he'd had to contend with. "Nora and I knew you could do it."

Reaching down, he touched my bulging belly, a tender smile on his face. "Nora? Really, are you sure?"

"I wouldn't have it any other way, naming her after your mom just seems right."

"It's perfect," he said, tears threatening to spill. "Hear that, Nora? Daddy is going to the playoffs!"

I laughed then, feeling deliriously happy at

all that life had brought me over the last few months. It was hard to even imagine what my life was before I'd bumped into Jacob and how unhappy I truly was.

"So," he said as I released him. "I had a bet and I'm going to make good on it."

"I thought you were done with bets," I teased, remembering the playbook that had brought us together in the most unconventional way. "Don't you know what kind of trouble they get you in?"

"I don't think I will have much problem with this one," he replied. Terrence suddenly appeared, thrust something into Jacob's hand and with a secretive grin backed away just as quickly.

Jacob dropped to one knee, and my stomach did a somersault. I felt the world around me fade out as I realized what he was doing. I was torn between wanting to tug him up and wanting to join him on my knees on the field. "Jacob, we don't have to do this."

"Oh yes we do, right here. Right now." He smiled, tenderness in his eyes. "I should have done this a long time ago but I wanted to prove to you that I had what it takes."

"Oh, Jacob, I always knew you did."

"Lucia, will you marry me?"

I looked down at him, biting my lip hard. I wanted to believe that he was doing this because he wanted to, but I had to be sure. "Did my father put you up to this?"

"Babe," he started, reaching out to grab my hand. "I want the world to know that you are mine. Marry me and put me out of my misery. Make me the happiest man alive, please?"

"Yes," I exclaimed, throwing my arms around his neck, all of my worry disappearing at his words. That was the Jacob I knew and loved. "Yes, I will marry you."

"Thank God," he laughed, picking me up as he rose from his knee. Clapping erupted, and I looked around, finding the entire team surrounding us—tiny explosions crackled as they all launched confetti over our heads.

"It's about time!" I heard a voice saying. They came around us, congratulating us, but between a couple of the players, I saw my father standing idly by. His face was full of happiness as he nodded his approval. I suspected the bet was between the two of them.

"You didn't even look at the ring," Jacob said, kissing me on the side of my neck before setting me down gently.

"I didn't need to. The look in your eyes told me

everything I need to know." He laughed and kissed me harder, causing everyone to cheer again.

"Would you still have done it if you'd lost?" I asked as we walked. "Propose, I mean?"

"Not on the field," he said, grabbing my hand and pulling me toward the locker room. "But yes, I would have done it tonight regardless. I can't wait to make you officially mine, and this is the first step, babe. I hope you are ready for this ride, because I don't plan to get off at any point." I grinned and laid my head on his shoulder. It was sinking in only now that he was mine, for real. I was very lucky indeed that he had found that playbook and chosen to pursue me.

Thank God for determined, arrogant football players, bad boys who didn't give up so easily.

Epilogue
JACOB

I awoke to someone shaking my shoulder. I took a moment to look around before I realized that Lucia's anxious face was peering down at me. Instantly I bolted up to a sitting position in our bed, gently grabbing the flesh of her bare arms to steady her. "What?" I asked hesitantly, a thousand thoughts running through my mind at what could be wrong. "What is it?"

She bit her lip, and I felt a wave of panic hit me. "I-I think my water broke."

It took one second for me to process what she was saying. "Right now? The baby? Fuck, the baby!"

She nodded and I released her carefully, pressing a gentle kiss on her forehead to show that I wasn't worried, at least externally. "Don't worry, we will be fine."

"I know," she sighed, climbing off of the bed, her swollen belly pale and tight in the moonlight. For the last month she had struggled to find a way to get a good night's sleep, trying everything from body pillows to sleeping naked. I had tried to help her as much as I could, even sleeping on the couch in the living room a few nights to give her all the space she needed. The funny thing was that we both ended up down there, unable to sleep apart. Thank God for an oversized sectional.

I climbed out of bed as I went through the checklist in my head. Bag. Check. Clothes on. Check. Wallet. Check. Charged camera. Check.

"Did you send out the text?" she asked as she struggled into a pair of loose pants on the other side of the room. "Doing it right now," I replied. With a little apprehension, I utilized the group text Lucia had set up in my phone a month earlier, updating the progress before shoving it into my pocket. Lucia slid a tank top over her head and then looked at me, tears in her eyes. "What if I can't do this, Jacob?"

I was at her side in a few steps, gathering her in my arms, her stomach between us. "You are the bravest person I know," I said softly, feeling my own heart break at the worry in her voice. I was a nervous wreck inside, scared to death that this day was finally here, and we would be seeing Nora in a few hours if everything went well. It was a terrifying feeling, but simultaneously exhilarating. But first, I had a pregnant wife to console. "Remember, you were brave enough to date a football player, putting everything on the line. That was far scarier, am I right?"

"Yeah, totally compares," she giggled, then hissed in pain. "I think the contractions are starting."

I immediately went into full-on boss mode, hiding my own anxiety as best I could. "Come on," I said. "As much as I want to see my daughter, I'd rather a doctor deliver her."

* * *

FOURTEEN HOURS LATER

I cringed as Lucia's dad barked into his phone for the hundredth time, his aide pacing with him as he walked the length of the waiting room. Merry and Cara were with Lucia now; we'd taken it in shifts to be in there with her. I had to do it this way—as much as I wanted to be in the delivery room all the time, I couldn't take the fact that Lucia was in so much pain and there was nothing I could do about it. I could see it on her face, hear it in her voice, and even with the epidural, she looked as if she were being ripped apart. It was tearing me up inside.

"I don't care what it takes! He's not getting the money, and that's final!" David hung up his phone and put it in his pocket, stopping abruptly. The aide sidestepped at the last moment to avoid running into his back and ended up falling into a chair as the new mayor of Jupiter turned back towards me, anxiety in his eyes, as well.

He'd only been in the mayor's office for a month, but I could tell he loved it, just like he loved owning the team. Me, I was just happy being his quarterback. Oh, and his son-in-law. Turns out it wasn't so bad being both. They had accepted me as part of the family with very little resistance, and for the first time in a long time, I felt like I belonged somewhere, with people who cared about my existence.

"Why is it taking so long?" he growled again, his eyes swinging to his aide, who seemed to be with him wherever he went. The young guy shrugged and I bit back a laugh, wondering if David would push him hard for an answer. Instead his eyes swung in my direction, and I found myself shrugging, as well.

"I don't know," I answered honestly. I had the same question. As each hour ticked by my blood pressure rose. During our classes, I'd learned that the birthing process could take fucking forever, so I was prepared. Kind of… just not for the torturous looks she kept giving me, like it was all my fault that she was in so much pain.

The door opened and Cara burst in, her eyes shining with tears. She had gone back about ten minutes ago, wanting to get an update and to get away from the growling men who were pacing the floors helplessly. I couldn't blame her.

"She's here!"

A weight that I didn't even know was there lifted off my shoulders, and I swallowed hard. "Sh-she's here? Lucia's okay?"

Cara nodded and then clapped me on the back. "Come on. Lucia wants you in that room pronto, Benchwarmer—you're up."

I gave her a look but didn't have time or thought process to throw her a retort. Instead I grinned and walked down the hall to the room, meeting Merry in the doorway, her eyes red but a happy expression on her face. "She's beautiful," she whispered, giving me a hug. "Congratulations, Jacob. You did a good job with this one."

I awkwardly patted her on the back and then entered the room, cautiously approaching the bed where Lucia lay. In her arms was a tiny bundle, wrapped tightly in a striped pink blanket. Our baby girl. Wow. I still couldn't believe it.

"Come here," she smiled, looking tired but gorgeous all at the same time. My heart filled with even more love for her then. "Meet your daughter."

My throat grew thick as I reached her side and took the bundle. My eyes filled with tears as I gazed down at the perfectly rose-colored face of my daughter for the first time. "Hello there, my little lovebug. She's gorgeous, absolutely perfect," I whispered. *I was a father.*

"That she is," Lucia answered as I carefully sat next to her, our shoulders brushing up against each other. "We did it, Jacob. Can you believe it? She's finally here, after all that waiting."

I looked over at her, and she wiped my wet cheeks with her hand, her own eyes shining with tears. "You did it. God, I love you so damn much."

"I know," she smiled, resting her head against my shoulder. "I love you too, Jacob."

I grinned then and looked back down to the wide-eyed baby in my arms, the daughter whom I was going to protect with my very life for as long as I was on this earth. "Do you think they make baby jerseys?"

Lucia laughed and ran her finger over the downy cheek of our beautiful little girl. "I think they do. Heck, I think we got some as gifts at the baby shower. But maybe we could get a championship jersey made?"

I nodded, unable to take my eyes off my daughter. My year had been fucking awesome. We had won the championship, and I was named MVP. Lucia and I had become engaged, then married, and I now was a proud daddy. I couldn't ask for much more. Leaning over, I pressed a kiss to Lucia's forehead, breathing in her scent as I did multiple times during the day whenever we were together.

Words couldn't describe the emotions I was feeling. She made me feel so proud to be by her side, so grateful that she had taken a chance on me—several in fact. And now we had a daughter between us and a future that was going to be so damn perfect that when I was old and crippled, I would still have this feeling in my chest that my life couldn't be any better. I had gone from a cocky football player who thought he had it all to a man who now knew that this was all he needed. And that was just fine by me.

Epilogue
LUCIA

I watched as Jacob drifted off to sleep, his jaw slack and the death grip he had on my hand now a bit lighter. He was so tired, and though he had been a trooper throughout the entire process, I knew he needed his rest. For the last hour we just sat here and enjoyed our little Nora, marveling at the miracle we had made together. It was still hard for me to believe that I was now a mom, that someone depended on me for the rest of my life. I was responsible for her, and the thought scared the shit out of me. And Jacob, as well. Though I could tell he was thrilled about her being here, I could see the worry in his eyes. Heck, I had the same in mine.

With a sigh, I leaned back on the pillow, exhausted. The birthing process had been a marathon of epic proportions. Now that all the excitement was over and she was finally here, I could feel the weariness starting to creep up in my body, urging me to get the rest while I could. My father and Merry couldn't be any prouder of their granddaughter, promising to have everything ready at the house when we'd come home. Auntie Cara was ecstatic, as well. I was very blessed to have such a good support system around Jacob and me.

Looking down, I noted that my wedding band wasn't as tight as it had been over the last few days. Thank God. It was a beautiful set, one that I had worn proudly until I couldn't get the square-cut engagement ring on anymore and was reduced to wearing just the sparkling band. Still, I couldn't imagine ever forgetting our wedding day.

It had been a small ceremony, taking place outdoors on my father's estate. The wedding dress was not what I had pictured growing up, but when you're six months preggo, you don't get the long, form-fitting gown. But I had still fallen in love with my choice.

I settled on a long and elegant lacy dress with an empire waist. And when my father walked me down the aisle the look of appreciation in Jacob's eyes was all I needed to reaffirm that the dress was a winner. The ceremony was beautiful and orderly, but the reception was far from quiet. The whole day seemed to echo our different personalities, the joining of two people who loved each other so much but who were quite opposite in so many ways. And I did. I loved Jacob with everything I had. He was my soulmate, my rock, and my best friend—though Cara would tell you otherwise—and I was extremely proud to be his wife.

Nora whimpered, and I laid a hand on her little body, glancing over at Jacob to ensure that he was still asleep. As much as I thought I wanted him in the delivery room, I could see that he was beside himself with worry. We'd made the quick decision to sub in Merry and Cara so he could gather himself. It was sweet of him to try and stay, but he looked like he was going to faint at any moment, and I shooed him away between pushes. Both Merry and Cara had been wonderful replacements.

But now our little family was together, and we had the world to take on. Jacob's performance was the best that it ever had been, and he was already touted to be the starter next season. And though I'd be on maternity leave, the practice was flourishing. I was now the consultant for a number of pro sports teams in the south, which couldn't make me happier. There was not one day that I regretted making that move.

"How are you still awake?" Jacob whispered and took my hand.

"Taking it all in, I guess. Planning, too. There's so much we need to do."

"Try and sleep, my love. Let me take care of you, of everything, okay? You've done enough for one day. Dream about our little girl and our future."

With a happy sigh and a nod, I closed my eyes, the day's events starting to catch up with me, comforted by the fact Jacob was taking charge.

"I love you, Mrs. Maddox," he said, caressing my hand. As I started to fall into a blissful sleep, I wondered if my dreams would show our futures, because I couldn't wait to see what life had in store for us next.

All about
EMILIA BEAUMONT

Emilia Beaumont is a full-time writer, originally hailing from England, living in the South of Ireland with her husband and a house full of cats. Surrounded by peaceful emerald fields she always has a pen and notebook to hand ready for when the next saucy idea strikes. Emilia is also an avid comic-book reader and a wildlife advocate.

www.emiliabeaumont.com
emilia@emiliabeaumont.com

Also by EMILIA BEAUMONT

FOR AN UP-TO-DATE LIST PLEASE VISIT:
WWW.EMILIABEAUMONT.COM/BOOKS

EXPECTING SERIES:

EXPECTING MY BILLIONAIRE STEPBROTHER'S BABY

LOVING MY BILLIONAIRE STEPBROTHER'S BABY

FORBIDDEN DESIRES SERIES:

SNAKE (A STEPBROTHER ROMANCE)

VULTURE (A STEPBROTHER ROMANCE)

SHARK (A STEPBROTHER ROMANCE)

DAMAGED SERIES:

THE PLAY BOOK (A BAD BOY SPORTS ROMANCE)

THE CURVE BALL (A BAD BOY SPORTS ROMANCE)

THE LOVE GAME (A BAD BOY SPORTS ROMANCE)

STAND ALONES:

BILLIONAIRE STEPBROTHER

KISS ME AGAIN (A SECOND CHANCE STEPBROTHER ROMANCE)

HITMAN'S REVENGE (A FORBIDDEN BAD BOY ROMANCE)

DREAM DADDY (A DADDY'S BEST FRIEND DARK ROMANCE)

DADDY EVER AFTER (A BILLIONAIRE ROMANCE)

ROYAL BASTARD (A BAD BOY ROYAL ROMANCE)

BAD BOY'S WEDDING

Made in the USA
Coppell, TX
08 August 2020